BLACK MAGIC
AT
BRILLSTONE

Florence Parry Heide
and Roxanne Heide

Cover and Frontispiece by
Joe Krush

ALBERT WHITMAN & COMPANY, *Chicago*

Library of Congress Cataloging in Publication Data
Heide, Florence Parry.
  Black magic at Brillstone.

  (Pilot Books)
  SUMMARY: Liza and Logan investigate a
spiritualist they believe is trying to cheat their
neighbor out of her inheritance.
  [1. Mystery and detective stories] I. Heide,
Roxanne, joint author. II. Krush, Joe. III. Title.
PZ7.H36Bl   [Fic]   81-487
ISBN 0-8075-0782-2   AACRI

3K13500001796C

People You'll Meet in
Black Magic at Brillstone
in the order they appear:

LOGAN FORREST, who lives at the Brillstone apartments. He enjoys his job as an auto mechanic almost as much as he enjoys delving into a mystery.

JENNY FORREST, Logan's mother, who shares a seventh floor apartment with him.

MISS VIOLET, a Brillstone resident who is charming, kind, and suddenly rich.

LOUIE, the manager of the Brillstone Apartments.

MRS. MERKLE, sometimes called MERK, who works as a housekeeper for some Brillstone tenants.

LIZA WEBSTER, Logan's friend, who can't resist a mystery. She and her father, WEBB, occupy the apartment just above Logan and Jenny's.

PHYLLIS BAKER, the representative of a proposed shelter for stray cats. She is seeking a donation from Miss Violet.

BELLA VINE, a spiritualist.

SAM WOOSER, formerly the manager of the Brillstone. Sam has returned for a visit.

Chapter One

Logan awoke suddenly, his eyes wide in the dark. There it was again, the sound he thought he had only dreamed. Someone was whistling "Mary Had a Little Lamb." Softly, eerily. And then he heard another sound. Someone was in the living room, quietly opening and closing the desk drawers.

Logan sat up and listened closely. It must be Jenny, his mother. But she never prowled around in the apartment late at night, and she never whistled. He smiled in the dark. Who was he to decide what his mother might or might not try next? He lay back on his pillow and stared at the ceiling.

Liza's bedroom was on the eighth floor of the Brillstone, just above his. The layout of the apartments was all the same. Of course, Liza and her father, Webb, had decorated theirs differently. The walls were painted in soft colors, and the furniture was old. Jenny had poured all that was light and bright and new into her and Logan's apartment. Logan couldn't decide which way he liked better. Each was right in itself, that was it. He felt just as at home in Liza and Webb's apartment as he did in his own. And he felt just as at home with them as he did with his mother, Jenny.

Logan turned over. The faint whistling stopped, then started again. What on earth was Jenny doing up at this hour? Probably she was as excited about seeing Webb as he was about seeing Liza. Three weeks was a long time for them to have been gone. And Seattle was a faraway place.

Logan propped himself up on an elbow and looked at the clock with the lighted face next to his bed. Three o'clock. In exactly twelve hours Liza and Webb would be landing at the airport. Logan sighed contentedly and turned over. They'd all have dinner here tomorrow night. Tonight, actually, he thought. Terrific.

The soft whistling of "Mary Had a Little Lamb" continued. Well, Jenny was awake, and so was he. He'd go in and keep her company.

Logan opened the door to his bedroom, but the living room was empty. He walked quietly to Jenny's bedroom door and opened it, peering in. He could hear her deep, steady breathing. She was sound asleep.

So it hadn't been Jenny, after all.

But then who had been whistling? And who had been opening and closing the desk drawers? Had it been a thief?

Logan picked up the telephone. He'd call the police. But halfway through dialing, he hesitated and set the phone down.

What would he say? Someone had been in the apartment whistling "Mary Had a Little Lamb"? That sounded so silly. Who would believe him?

He studied the desk, then opened and closed each drawer. Nothing seemed to be missing. He checked the front door. It was locked. No one without a key could have come in.

He glanced at the glass door that led to the balcony. Was someone out there, hiding? Taking a deep breath, he walked over. But the balcony door was locked, too.

As Logan turned and surveyed the living room once again, his eyes lighted on the cart he had borrowed from Louie, the Brillstone manager. Logan had taken all of Liza's plants and had repotted them. Now they stood on Louie's cart, ready to be returned to Liza's apartment in the morning. He wished Liza were here now. He really missed her.

Logan went back to his room and lay in bed, trying to feel drowsy. But the memory of the strange whistling and the sound of the drawers being opened and closed stayed with him and kept him awake. When his alarm went off, his eyes were wide open.

By the time he had showered and dressed, Jenny was up, too. She was at the kitchen table, reading the morning paper and sipping coffee.

Logan wondered with a sharp pang of guilt if he should have followed through with that call to the police. Well, if the same thing ever happened again, he would.

Jenny smiled at him and took a last gulp of coffee. "I'm off in a cloud of dust," she said, glancing out the window. "In a cloud of fog, I should say. Let's hope it doesn't get any worse and delay Webb and Liza's flight home."

Logan looked out the window. The fog was so thick, he could hardly see the ground. He crossed his fingers, hoping that it wouldn't get any thicker—at least not until after Liza and Webb's plane had landed.

Jenny took her purse from the chair. "Dinner for tonight is in the Crockpot."

"I'll make the salad dressing when I get back from work," Logan offered.

"Everybody should have somebody like you," said Jenny. She blew a kiss as she walked out of the apartment.

Logan put a couple of crisp strips of bacon on a buttered piece of toast as he listened to the weather report on the radio. More fog was predicted. He drained the last of his milk. Yes, he had the key to Liza and Webb's apartment, and yes, he had his car keys, and yes, he was excited about tonight. He'd take the cart of plants up to Liza's now.

Logan opened the door and carefully wheeled the borrowed cart out to the corridor. He locked the door, frowning as he thought about the invisible guest of the night before and the whistled tune of "Mary Had a Little Lamb." Eerie.

"Oh, it's you," called a soft voice from across the hall. Miss Violet, an elderly tenant of the Brillstone, stood in the doorway of her apartment. She held her cat, who licked his paws slowly and methodically. "I heard someone coming, and I thought it was my expected guest, Bella Vine." She glanced at the cart laden with plants. "For Liza?"

Logan nodded. "She'll be home tonight."

"Oh, I know," said Miss Violet, pushing a white strand of hair into a tuft of other white hairs. "I've been counting the days, just as I imagine you have." Her blue eyes twinkled as she rearranged a blue scarf around her neck. Logan felt himself redden. Did everyone in the world know how he felt about Liza?

"I have missed that girl sorely," Miss Violet went on. "With her away, most of my projects are just lying dormant. We have so much to catch up on." She stroked her cat. "Haven't we, Bainbridge?"

Miss Violet was wearing a bright blue blouse and long white skirt. A wide red cummerbund was around her tiny waist. She always dressed in various combinations of red, white, and blue. Her apartment was decorated in red, white, and blue, as well, Logan thought. He smiled.

"Would you do me a great favor, Logan? Not that I want to interfere in the teeniest way with your evening. But could you ask Liza to just pop her head in after supper? I have some things I absolutely must have her sort through before she comes over tomorrow for our work session."

"I'll tell her," Logan promised. He started to push the cart past Miss Violet's doorway toward the elevators.

"I'm just going to wait here for Bella Vine," Miss Violet said.

Whoever *she* was, thought Logan. Miss Violet always seemed to have lots of guests coming and going.

He started down the corridor, thinking again about the strange guest in his own apartment. He began to whistle "Mary Had a Little Lamb" under his breath, the way he had heard it in the night.

"If I didn't know better," came the small voice of Miss Violet, "I'd say you were my nephew, Jessie."

Logan stared back at her.

"He always whistled through his teeth, even when he was a little boy. Just the way you were whistling. And he always whistled 'Mary Had a Little Lamb.' But he never even knew he was doing it. It was a terrible habit." She shook her head, smiling. "Even on very solemn occasions. Once he even whistled in church during the Easter service. It was very embarrassing."

Miss Violet rubbed her cat behind the ears. "'Mary Had a Little Lamb.' Only he always would say that he was really whistling 'Violet Had a Little Cat.' I think that if you have a nervous habit—something you can't help doing and don't even *know* you're doing—that it should be something silent, don't you agree?"

Logan smiled. But he was worried. Could Miss Violet's nephew, Jessie, have broken into the apartment in the middle of the night? How would he have managed to get in? And why would he have come? What could he have been looking for?

"I've always adored cats," Miss Violet went on. "And I've always had one. Nearly always. But only one at a time, so that it's just the cat and me. You develop the best relationships that way, you know."

She looked down the corridor. "It's not like Bella Vine to be late. But, then, she's a spiritualist," she added. "Maybe spiritualists lose track of time sometimes—they have so many other things to think about."

A spiritualist! That didn't sound like Miss Violet, thought Logan. She didn't seem like the type to believe in communicating with the dead.

"It's very foggy," he said. "Maybe she's been delayed because of the weather."

"Of course, that's it," agreed Miss Violet. "Well, as I said, if I didn't know better, I'd have thought you were my nephew, Jessie, whistling 'Mary Had a Little Lamb.'"

Logan stood there, confused. *Why* or *how* would Miss Violet's nephew, Jessie, have entered the apartment? It didn't make sense.

Well, he'd have to worry later. He had to deliver the cart with the plants to Liza's apartment and then go to work at the garage.

"I'll tell Liza you want to see her after supper," he said, guiding the cart along the corridor to the elevators. He pressed the button and waited.

When the doors opened, Logan started to back the cart into the elevator.

"Whoa there," said Louie, the manager of the Brillstone Apartments. "You nearly got me that time."

He was holding a big bouquet of roses.

"Sorry, Louie," Logan apologized. "I'm all thumbs today."

"Green thumbs, then," said Louie, admiring the array of plants on the cart. "You did a good job with Liza's plants. Bet you'll be glad to see her tonight, right?"

"Right," said Logan. Did he really wear his heart on his sleeve?

"Hey," said Louie. "If you're going up to Liza's now, would you do me a favor and take these flowers with you? They were just delivered, and let me tell you, it's one rat race down in the lobby. People are calling for their cleaning to be delivered, their groceries—because of the fog, you know. I just caught the latest weather report, and I'm sure everybody else did, too. Nobody is taking any chances out there." He glanced at the bouquet in his hand. "You wouldn't mind carrying these up? I'm swamped."

"Sure, I'll take them," Logan said.

"Thanks." Louie stepped out of the elevator before the doors closed. "I hate leaving the lobby when it's so busy. Besides, I've got to call the elevator people. That other elevator is acting up again. Hope it gets me down to the lobby." The doors swished shut on Louie's last word.

Logan looked at the bouquet in his hand. Roses for Liza. A small card was stapled to the green paper. "Miss you already. Dan."

Logan looked at the card again as the elevator doors slid open. Who was Dan, anyway? Someone Liza had met in Seattle?

Logan wheeled the cart off the elevator and glanced down at the plants he had repotted. They didn't seem as impressive now.

He pulled out Liza's key and opened the door, then wheeled the cart into the apartment. Mrs. Merkle, a housekeeper who helped many of the Brillstone tenants, was cleaning the glass door that led to the balcony. "Well, it's Logan, and it's the plants! They look terrific, all in new skins. Want me to put them back where they belong?"

"That would be great," nodded Logan. "I forgot where they go."

She glanced at the big bouquet of roses that Logan held. "You got her roses, too? Ah, Logan, you are the romantic one."

"I didn't get her the roses, Merk," Logan said.

She studied the bouquet and the card. "Well, I'll get a vase," she decided. "Plants are nicer than cut flowers, anyway, Logan. Roses are a nuisance.

Never did like them, myself." She took the flowers out to the kitchen.

Logan glanced around the living room, aware once again of how different his apartment and Liza's were. "You really have everything sparkled up, Merk," he said. "The place looks great!"

"Webb and Liza deserve the best, right?" she called from the kitchen. In a moment she came back in. With impressive speed and efficiency, she picked up two plants at a time and set them in their proper places. "I told your mom I'd bake a cake and leave it at your apartment for tonight. I know she hates fussing with desserts."

"You're one in a million, Merk!"

"You probably say that to all the girls," she said, going back to the big glass door.

Logan wheeled the empty cart out of the apartment and returned it to Louie's storage room. Then he headed for work. The fog had not lifted, but he made it to the garage on time.

Ordinarily Logan loved his job. Working on cars was one of his favorite things. But today every minute that ticked by seemed to last an hour.

When it was closing time, Logan took off his grease-stained smock and hurried to his car.

The fog still hung over the city, and traffic was

slow. Logan flicked on the radio, hoping for some word about the airport.

He smiled with relief when the announcement came on: the airport had not closed until 4:30. That meant Liza and Webb had probably been able to land.

Logan parked his car in the underground garage at the Brillstone, then hurried to the elevators. He got there just before the doors closed. Several passengers were already inside.

Logan faced the front of the elevator and thought about the evening ahead. Maybe he should make a welcome home sign. Yes. And tape it to the kitchen door.

Suddenly the elevator jerked to a stop. The lights went out.

"Oh no, not again," moaned a passenger.

A series of nervous coughs and sighs followed. Clunking noises came from somewhere high in the elevator shaft.

And then Logan felt the hair on the back of his neck stand on end. Behind him in the dark he heard the same tune he had heard the night before. Someone was whistling "Mary Had a Little Lamb," softly, eerily.

Was Miss Violet's nephew, Jessie, standing

behind him in the elevator at this very moment?

The elevator started moving again, and soon the doors swished open on Logan's floor. He stepped out, turning around to see who was whistling. But the elevator was still dark, and he couldn't pick out any faces.

Logan turned slowly and walked down the corridor to his apartment. The person in the elevator—and in his apartment—must have been Jessie, the nephew Miss Violet had mentioned this morning. Who else would have whistled like that? But how—and why—had Jessie come into Logan and Jenny's apartment last night? What had he wanted?

Logan reached his apartment and checked the door before he put in his key. Of course, it was locked. He hesitated a moment longer, then walked in. It was hard to shake off the feeling that someone was in the apartment. He hoped that Liza would come down soon. He needed her.

Logan showered and dressed. Then he walked briskly to the kitchen. He'd promised Jenny that he'd make the salad dressing. It was a trick he'd learned from Webb. As he turned on the blender, he remembered the welcome home sign he was going to make for Liza and Webb. He'd better check to see whether Jenny still had all those colored pencils and the poster board.

He started into the living room, catching a movement out of the corner of his eye. He stood stock-still.

The apartment door was slowly being pulled shut.

Logan stared, his throat suddenly dry. Then he ran to the door and yanked it open.

There was not a soul in sight. Not a shadow, not a whisper of movement.

Logan swallowed, aware of his heart thudding in his chest. He shut the door—unsure what his next move should be. Something strange— something spooky—was going on at the Brillstone.

A few moments later, Jenny rushed into the apartment. "That fog, Logan!" she exclaimed. "It's terrible. But I checked with the airlines. Liza and Webb's plane did land. They'll probably be knocking at our door in ten minutes. Excited?"

"Sort of," Logan said. "Sort of very." He smiled at his mother, trying to conceal his worry.

He knew he'd have to tell her about the mysterious intruder of last night and this afternoon. Something far too strange was going on to be silent about it. But there wasn't time to talk now, and he didn't want to spoil Webb and Liza's homecoming.

"Let's share the chores," Jenny said. "You set the table, and I'll take the fastest shower on record and put on something absolutely smashing that I bought just for the occasion."

Logan resisted the impulse to telephone upstairs to Liza. After all, she'd be here in a few minutes. He set the table, then made and taped up the welcome sign. When he heard the familiar knock at the door—three shorts and two longs—he took a deep breath and pulled the door open.

There were Webb and Liza, smiling their old familiar smiles.

Logan found that no words came. He could have kicked himself.

Liza finally said "Hi." Her voice was almost inaudible.

Then, as if magically, the tension disappeared and everyone started to talk at once.

"Logan! My plants! They look elegant in their new pots. What a wonderful surprise!"

"Webb, I can see that you adored Seattle," said Jenny, giving him a hug.

"Not as much as I adore getting home."

Everything was the same, Logan realized. No, not everything. Liza looked wonderful—but different. What was it?

Jenny answered his unspoken question. "Liza, I love your new hairdo!"

"I thought it would make me look older," Liza confessed.

Logan studied Liza's face. Why would she want to look older? For this Dan somebody? Was he older? Logan didn't want to think about that. Not now. He wanted to get back on his and Liza's old footing. And he wanted to tell her and Webb and Jenny about the strange things that had been happening at the Brillstone.

"It's good to be back," admitted Liza. "Obviously everything falls apart when we're gone. Take that crazy elevator. Dad and I nearly had cardiac arrest coming up with our luggage. The lights went out, and the elevator stopped between floors. It was like a late-late movie."

"We've had trouble with the elevator all week," said Jenny. "But Louie absolutely, positively guarantees that it will be fixed by tomorrow."

"The same thing happened when I was on the elevator after work this afternoon," said Logan.

"And then someone behind me started to whistle 'Mary Had a Little Lamb.' It was spooky."

"What's so spooky about an old nursery rhyme?" Liza asked.

Logan hesitated. "Someone was in our living room in the middle of the night last night. Whoever it was opened and closed the desk drawers and whistled 'Mary Had a Little Lamb.'"

He turned to Jenny. "I didn't want to scare you, Mom, so I didn't say anything to you. But I think that it's better if everything is out in the open."

Jenny raised her eyebrows and stared at Logan. "Someone in our apartment? Whistling?"

Logan nodded. "Actually, I'm pretty positive that it was Miss Violet's nephew, Jessie. But I can't figure out why or how he'd come into our apartment in the night."

Webb put down his coffee cup. "But Jessie's been dead for five years," he said slowly.

Chapter Two

Dead!" echoed Logan. "But I was sure it was Jessie in the apartment early this morning and in the elevator whistling 'Mary Had a Little Lamb.'"

"In this country, Logan, anyone can whistle anything they want to," Liza joked.

"Not in my apartment," Logan told her, smiling.

"Who was Jessie, anyway?" Liza asked.

Webb answered. "Miss Violet's only nephew. And her only living relative."

"It was a sad thing," Jenny said. "Jessie had gone over to some broken-down hotel, which was patronized mostly by bums. Derelicts. His wife said later that he had taken over some old clothes he'd wanted to give them. Anyway, there was a fire, and everyone was lost.

"That's terrible!" said Liza. "And how sad for Jessie's wife and for Miss Violet."

"Yes," said Webb. "I never knew the wife, and she moved away right after the funeral. As for Miss Violet, I don't think she and Jessie were close, but after all, he was her sister's son."

Logan leaned back, thinking. It couldn't have been Jessie, then, in the apartment early this morning. But it had been someone. Someone who had opened and closed the desk drawers. Someone who had whistled "Mary Had a Little Lamb."

Or "Violet Had a Little Cat."

The same tune Jessie whistled.

"I really like Miss Violet," said Liza.

"I think everyone does," agreed Webb, rubbing the bowl of his cold pipe. "She's a nice person. Maybe too nice."

"What's that supposed to mean?" asked Liza. "Too nice?"

"Miss Violet is a lovely lady—sweet and kind, as we all know." Webb paused and frowned. "It seems that an old, old friend of hers from England, Annie Banderly, recently died and left her some money."

"Money?" sighed Logan. "Now there's something I haven't seen lately."

Liza leaned forward. "Has Miss Violet come into a lot of money, Dad?"

Webb nodded. "Yes, quite a lot."

"That's terrific," Liza declared.

"Webb's not so sure about that," said Jenny, glancing at him. "He's afraid that people will take advantage of her."

Webb tapped the stem of his pipe with his thumb. "Miss Violet feels that since she already has enough to live on, she should give away her inheritance. And she thinks she should give it away now, not after she dies."

Logan raised his eyebrows. "Give it away to who? To what?"

"She wants to give the money to a good cause," Webb explained. "There are always enough of those, of course. But for every good cause there's a phony one. For every sincere person wanting the money, there's an unscrupulous or dishonest one."

Jenny smiled at Webb. "Of course, everyone with any cause of any kind has heard about Miss Violet's inheritance. It was mentioned in all the newspapers."

"How can she tell the difference between good causes and phony ones?" asked Liza.

"I'll check out the ones that she seems to be serious about," Webb explained. "For example, Miss Violet is very interested in establishing a home for stray cats. That's always been one of her concerns. There are so many homeless, hungry cats."

"And someone wants her to give the money to cats?" asked Liza.

Webb rubbed his chin. "To a home for cats," he said. "It's called, whimsically, 'the Cat's Meow.'"

Liza made a face.

"It's a not-for-profit corporation," Webb went on. "It's been recently incorporated. The organizers need money in order to build the shelter. Miss Violet's financial contribution would make that possible. It would also provide enough income for the shelter to continue for many, many years."

"A cat shelter," said Logan. "It sounds funny to me."

"That's because you're not terribly fond of cats," said Jenny. "Since Miss Violet is, it doesn't seem very funny to her to give a great deal of money to a home for homeless cats."

Webb smiled. "I'll look at some of the

information tonight when the representative of the shelter stops by. Miss Violet called me just as we got back from the airport, Jenny. She asked if I would be willing to talk to Phyllis Baker, the representative, about the shelter. Miss Violet is having an interview with her this evening, and I suggested that Phyllis Baker come over here afterwards. I hope that's all right."

"Of course," said Jenny. "Besides, I'm curious about the cat shelter, myself."

Webb set his pipe down. "I've urged Miss Violet not to do anything too quickly, but she is very eager to give the money away. As she says, the sooner she gives it, the sooner it can be spent for a worthy cause. And, of course, one can't quarrel with that reasoning."

"Webb wants to protect her from the wrong people and the fake causes," Jenny explained to Logan and Liza. "He's tried to persuade Miss Violet to let him visit with the people who have made proposals." She smiled ruefully. "But not all of these people have been interested in talking to Webb. Some of them claim to be too busy. Like Bella Vine."

"Tell them about her," suggested Webb.

Logan blinked. Bella Vine. The name rang a

bell. Then he remembered. Miss Violet had been waiting for her this morning.

"Okay," agreed Jenny. "Now hear this. Bella Vine is a spiritual advisor."

"A spiritual advisor?" Liza raised her eyebrows. "What's that?"

Jenny shrugged. "Your guess is as good as mine. This is the picture. Miss Violet's old friend in England, Annie Banderly, was a strong believer in the spirit world. She believed that living people could communicate with the dead, through a medium or spiritualist."

Liza's eyes widened.

"And so now Miss Violet believes that, too?"

Jenny shrugged again. "I don't know. But I do know that Bella Vine has been visiting Miss Violet often lately."

Webb cleared his throat. "I'm sure Bella Vine is probably sincere. She's in an organization of spiritualists—what's it called, Jenny?—the Seekers, isn't it? Miss Violet may decide to give her inherited money to them because of her friend's belief in spiritualism."

Logan frowned. Some strange things were going on in the Brillstone. Jessie, whistling "Mary Had a Little Lamb." Jessie, opening and closing drawers in the middle of the night. Jessie, dead. And a spiritualist visiting Miss Violet.

Liza spoke up indignantly. "This Bella Vine probably wants to make sure Miss Violet's money goes to the Seekers instead of to the poor stray cats."

Webb smiled at her affectionately. "Naturally, people think that their own causes are the most important ones. And perhaps all of the causes Miss Violet is considering are important. It's up to her to decide, of course. It's her money, after all."

Liza and Logan stood up and started to clear away the empty plates.

"A home for stray cats," he muttered on the way out to the kitchen. "I still think there's something fishy about it."

"Well, Dad says the representative of the shelter is coming over. We can see for ourselves whether she looks evil. Dad never suspects anyone of doing anything wrong."

"Neither does Mom," said Logan.

There was a knock at the door. "Speak of the devil," he said. "That must be Phyllis Baker now."

Logan opened the door.

A slim woman about his height stood smiling in the doorway, her hand outstretched. "I'm Phyllis Baker," she said. "I understand from Miss Violet that Mr. Webster wants to talk with me about our proposed shelter for stray cats."

"Come in," said Logan. As he shook her hand, he thought how much you could tell about people from their handshakes. Phyllis Baker's was as firm as his. That was a good sign, he decided.

She walked purposefully into the living room. Logan wondered how anyone could balance on such high heels, but Phyllis Baker looked as natural and graceful as anyone he'd ever seen. Her short pale hair bounced as she nodded to Webb's offer to sit down. She placed her enormous briefcase next to her.

"I'm so glad to have an opportunity to talk with you about our proposal," she said warmly. With a businesslike air, she pulled out a couple of brochures and handed them to Webb.

"Miss Violet, as you know, has a strong interest in protecting and sheltering stray, hungry, and homeless cats," she said in a crisp voice. "I think you will find that this proposed shelter is an exceptionally fine plan."

Webb nodded and glanced through the

brochures. He started to ask a question, but the telephone interrupted him.

Logan picked up the receiver.

It was Louie. "There's a package down here, just arrived, for Liza. I figured she'd be at your place. Want to run on down and pick it up?"

Logan and Liza excused themselves from the living room and hurried down to the lobby. Louie smiled and waved when he saw them.

"Here's your package," he said, reaching under his desk. "It's a curious one, all right. And cold, too." He brought up a medium-sized package. "It says 'Refrigerate immediately,' so I guess you should. Incidentally, you'll be glad to know the elevator's finally been fixed."

Liza took the heavily insulated package and stared at it. Logan stared, too. The postmark said "Seattle." "Jimmy's Wharf, the Best on the Sound" was written across the top in black lettering.

Seattle. Logan frowned. Was this something else from Dan?

When Liza and Logan reached the elevators, she groaned. "Now what?" she asked, looking up at the dial. It showed that one of the elevators was stuck between two floors.

"And Louie said everything had been fixed," she grumbled.

"Let's walk," suggested Logan.

Liza agreed. "The elevators must be haunted," she said. "Like your apartment, with that whistling in the middle of the night."

They started to walk up to the seventh floor. "That really was strange," said Logan. He shifted the package to his other arm. "Who could the whistler have been?"

"Jessie's ghost," said Liza promptly. "Or someone pretending to be Jessie's ghost." She paused at the landing. "Look, Logan. Nobody would come into an apartment in the middle of the night and start whistling without wanting to be heard."

"Unless it was just a nervous habit," Logan said. "Miss Violet told me Jessie couldn't help whistling."

"But he's dead. And it seems very, very unlikely that someone else would have exactly the same habit and exactly the same melody, 'Mary Had a Little Lamb.' The intruder is probably someone who wanted to make you *think* that you heard Jessie's ghost."

Logan smiled and started up the stairs to the

next floor. "Whoever it was picked the wrong guy to fool," he said. "I don't believe in ghosts."

"Neither do I, of course," said Liza quickly. "But the things that have been happening around here are really spooky. Why would anyone want you to believe in a ghost?"

"Maybe if I was convinced, then I could help convince Miss Violet," said Logan. "And if Miss Violet believed in a ghost, maybe she'd give her money to that spiritualist."

"Bella Vine," said Liza slowly. "Maybe it was Bella Vine who came into your apartment. Maybe she wants to convince you—and Miss Violet—that there are ghosts around here."

"I wonder," said Logan.

When he and Liza reached his apartment, Phyllis Baker was gone.

"She left a few minutes ago," said Webb. "I'll have other opportunities to visit with her unless Miss Violet suddenly makes a decision." He looked at Liza's package. "What have you got?"

"I don't know," Liza answered. "Let's find out." Logan set the box down on the coffee table. He slit the top open with his pocket knife. Liza peered into the package. She looked puzzled for a moment, then burst out laughing.

A large frozen fish, wrapped in plastic, lay inside.

"A fish?" Logan said.

"A steelhead," Liza said. "Fishing for them is very popular in Seattle."

"Oh," Logan said. He watched as Liza opened a letter taped to the outside of the box. Her cheeks flushed, and she quickly stuffed the letter back into the envelope.

"Who's it from?" Logan asked nonchalantly.

"Oh, just someone Dad and I met in Seattle," Liza answered.

Logan thought of the roses and the message— "Miss you already. Dan." Who was this Dan, anyway? And how did Liza feel about him?

"Well, I'd better get the fish into the freezer," Liza said. "I'll use yours, Logan, while we do the dishes."

Logan watched glumly as Liza placed the fish in the freezer.

After they had cleaned up the kitchen, they found Webb and Jenny in the living room, talking about the cat shelter.

"Everything seems to be on the up and up," said Webb, pouring himself a cup of coffee. "Of course, the group has no money at present, just a charter and their rather impressive plans. The shelter will be built as the money comes in."

"Do you think Miss Violet will give them the money she inherited from Annie Banderly?" asked Liza.

"She may," said Webb. "It's the sort of charity she has always favored."

Liza blew a kiss as she and Logan headed out the door to Miss Violet's apartment.

"The cat shelter sounds a lot better than the spiritualist group," said Liza.

"They both sound strange to me," said Logan.

Chapter Three

Logan and Liza knocked on Miss Violet's door. As she opened it, an odor of incense drifted toward them.

"How glad I am to see you again, my dear!" Miss Violet said. "And of course, you, too, Logan."

Logan looked over Miss Violet's shoulder. Someone else was in the apartment. A woman with thick, cascading black hair and layers of odd clothing stood quietly in a corner of the living room. Her black eyebrows arched above heavily mascaraed eyelashes, and her mouth was large and crimson. Around her thick waist was a braided belt with tassels. She held a red bowl with a stick of incense burning in it.

"You must meet Bella Vine," said Miss Violet.

The woman waved the incense in front of her. Her bracelets clanged.

"I'm moved to meet both of you," she said softly, with a slight Southern accent. "Forgive me if I don't shake your hands on the first meeting. It takes me a moment or two to place your auras and get a reading. The distance today will be made up a thousandfold later." She closed her eyes and bowed her head. A purple veil swung to her shoulders.

Miss Violet smiled almost apologetically. "I don't want you two to think that I'm taken in by silly things like ghosts and poltergeists and such, but I want to have an open mind. After all, my dear departed Annie saw something worthwhile in the world of the spirit."

Logan could see why Webb had been concerned. This Bella Vine seemed a strange character. Would she be able to convince Miss Violet to leave her money to the spiritual organization? Logan tried to remember the name. The Seekers, that was it.

"Poltergeists?" Liza asked. "What are they?"

Miss Violet smoothed her hair. "I believe they're those nasty little ghosts that bang things around, throw dishes, and rip pictures off walls. They're only in books, of course."

"Not so, our Miss Violet," came Bella Vine's

quiet voice. She slowly waved the incense about her.

"Indeed, it is true that poltergeists are energetic little spirits and make themselves known by being somewhat noisy. But they're not just in books—oh no, indeed, our Miss Violet. Documented case histories abound in the United States as well as in England, where your dear Annie lived a full and spirit-filled life." She paused and breathed deeply.

"Well," Miss Violet said briskly, "perhaps we can bring this up later." She smiled at Liza. "We were having a session, dear, before you and Logan came over. Bella Vine believes that we must have incense on occasions like this to—what was it?— to dispel the worldly odors of mortal living." She shook her head. "I am a difficult student but, at least, an earnest one."

Miss Violet reached down and picked up her cat. "You're going to be very proud of me, Liza," she announced. "While you were gone, I threw away a huge pile of things I never want to see again. And I put in a big box all the things worth keeping—old clippings and letters and whatnot that are very important to me. We can finish my scrapbook now, Liza!"

"That's wonderful," said Liza.

"And the best part of all," Miss Violet went on, "is that I've cleaned out every single thing from the living-room desk and have nothing but the snapshots in those drawers. This means, my dear, that we can finish identifying and labeling the pictures, as well. I'm really eager to complete the project."

"So am I," said Liza. It was fun to hear Miss Violet's reminiscences, fun to piece together the bits and scraps of her colorful life. Having traveled around the world several times, Miss Violet had decided to compile mementos from her past. Perhaps she might even write a book, she had told Liza. The pictures interested Liza most. She was eager to see more of the people Miss Violet had been telling her about.

Miss Violet clapped her hands excitedly. "I could never do it alone, Liza. A memory project calls for another to share it, don't you agree?"

Liza nodded.

"I'll get the box," declared Miss Violet, gently setting her small cat down.

Bella Vine cooed to the cat. As he brushed against her heavy skirt, she smiled.

In a moment Miss Violet carried in a box filled

with loose newspaper articles and letters. "Liza, why don't you just look these over for a minute before you go, to see whether you have any questions." She glanced at Logan. "I promised your young man I wouldn't make you do a thing tonight, but—"

"I'd be glad to look through the material, Miss Violet," said Liza.

Bella Vine remained in the corner of the living room. Her arms moved back and forth as she waved the burning incense.

Liza sat cross-legged on the floor and started sorting through the things in the box. Logan joined her.

Suddenly the telephone rang, and Miss Violet answered it. "Sam!" she exclaimed. "Oh, indeed, it was so nice to see you this afternoon, after all these years."

She paused, listening, absently tucking strands of her white hair back into place. "No, Sam, I simply can't reach any decisions yet. Having all this money to dispose of is a great responsibility, you know. I have to think everything through very, very carefully. I can't let my emotions sway me entirely, you know."

She frowned. "Yes, Sam, of course. Yes, you

may stop by later. But we will have to talk over your proposal another time."

She turned away from the telephone. "A dear man, Sam Wooser. He used to work here at the Brillstone many years ago. Before your time, Liza. Or yours, Logan. And to think he's back for a visit! A sentimental journey, he calls it." She paused. "He was delighted to read about my inheritance. Imagine, people hearing about it way out in Arizona!"

Logan glanced over at Bella Vine. Under half-closed lids, she was watching Miss Violet.

Liza stood up with the box. "I can't think of any questions, Miss Violet. I'll have everything sorted and arranged before I come down for our work session tomorrow afternoon."

"I feel comfortable about your auras," came Bella Vine's soft voice from the corner. "Perhaps another time we can delve more deeply into each other's spiritual space."

Out in the hallway, Logan took a deep breath. "Let's take the box up to your apartment and talk. That will give Webb and Jenny some time alone to catch up, and us, too."

Liza nodded. They reached her apartment and let themselves in.

She put the box down on the couch and sat down beside it. "Auras! Spiritual space! Let's hope Bella Vine doesn't hypnotize Miss Violet into leaving her money to her and her oddball group, the Seekers."

"And that Sam Wooser seems to be trying to talk her into something, too," said Logan. He reached for a pretzel and munched on it thoughtfully. "A lot of funny things have been going on," he said. "For instance, someone got into our apartment, opened and closed drawers, whistled, and disappeared into thin air. The same character was on the elevator with me after work when the lights went off. He whistled the same tune—Jessie's tune, 'Mary Had a Little Lamb.' And another strange thing happened this afternoon. I forgot to tell you about it, but someone came into my apartment after I got home from work. I looked up and saw the door closing. But when I checked the hall, no one was in sight. No one."

Liza leaned back on the couch. "A lot of coincidences," she agreed. "Miss Violet inherits a large sum of money. Then suddenly Bella Vine starts coming to visit her. And Sam Wooser appears after years away. And someone goes around whistling to spook people."

Logan looked thoughtfully over at Liza. "Someone is trying to make people believe in a ghost—Jessie's ghost."

Liza nodded. "I think that someone is Bella Vine."

"Maybe," said Logan, frowning. "Unless a couple of playful poltergeists are just playing tricks." He reached for another pretzel. "I wonder if poltergeists can open and close drawers. And whistle."

When Logan left Liza's apartment, he couldn't get his mind off Bella Vine. Could she *really* be behind all the strange things that were happening at the Brillstone? She was a character, all right, with her odd clothing and incense and her strange way of talking. Well, she was a spiritualist, the only one Logan had ever met. Maybe they were all like that.

Logan walked down the back stairs to his apartment. As he opened the door to the seventh-floor hallway, he was startled to see Bella Vine standing at the far end. She was not alone. A tall, stooped, gray-haired man was with her. The two seemed to be talking quietly.

Logan frowned and then turned to his own

apartment. As he took his key out of his pocket, he saw Bella Vine start toward the elevator, her long skirts rustling and her big, soft bag swinging clumsily. She did not look around.

Logan hesitated, his hand on his apartment door. Behind him, the tall man knocked at Miss Violet's.

"Come in, Sam," said Miss Violet.

So that was Sam Wooser!

And then the corridor was empty, except for Logan. He let himself into his apartment. Jenny and Webb had gone out.

As Logan got ready for bed, he thought about Bella Vine. What was her connection with Sam Wooser? Were they plotting something—some way to get Miss Violet's inheritance?

Was Sam in cahoots with the spiritualist, Bella Vine? Could he have pretended to be Jessie's ghost? Or was it just a coincidence that Sam and Bella Vine had been talking together?

Logan tried to sleep but couldn't. It was impossible to shake the feeling that Sam Wooser and Bella Vine were working together—trying to fool Miss Violet, to cheat her out of her money.

Chapter Four

The next morning Liza busied herself with the box of clippings and letters. She arranged them all chronologically and copied some of the important dates in the calendar she and Miss Violet had put together. The calendar of her life, Miss Violet called it. There were some letters without envelopes and dates. She'd have to ask Miss Violet about those right away. Then Liza could have everything organized before their time together this afternoon.

Liza put the letters in an envelope and ran down the stairs. When Miss Violet opened the door, Liza saw Phyllis Baker seated on the couch, her trim legs crossed at the ankles. Miss Violet's cat was perched on the back of the couch behind her.

"I'm so excited about our projects, Liza," said Miss Violet. She turned to Phyllis Baker. "You two have met?" They both nodded. "Liza is organizing me, you know. She's putting all of the meaningful clippings and letters of my life into a huge scrapbook, in chronological order. Then I can leaf through the scrapbook, and it will be like leafing through my whole life. Isn't that wonderful?"

Phyllis Baker smiled at Miss Violet. "Everyone should do that, really," she said. "But most of us lose or throw away the things we should have saved."

Miss Violet nodded. "I'm only saving the important ones. The milestones." She took the envelope from Liza and carried it over to the desk. "I'll just put the dates on these letters, Liza. I'm sure I can remember when they were written." She pulled a tiny blue chair up to the desk and started to work.

Liza turned to Phyllis Baker. "The shelter for stray cats sounds interesting," she said.

"It's going to be one of the finest in the country," said Phyllis Baker. "We are very fortunate to have someone like Miss Violet interested in our project."

Miss Violet lifted her head. "I won't deny it. I'm terribly interested, Miss Baker. I wish I could give you an answer right now, but my conscience just won't let me. I'll need a little more time. There are other important causes clamoring for attention."

"Of course, Miss Violet."

Miss Violet stood up and held the letters out to Liza. "All dated, Liza. I couldn't forget these particular letters, ever."

Liza went back up to her own apartment and worked the rest of the morning on Miss Violet's project. Later, as she fixed herself a chicken salad sandwich, she thought about Phyllis Baker's cat shelter. Stray cats were one of Miss Violet's special interests. As for Bella Vine and her spiritualist group—Liza shook her head worriedly.

By three o'clock Liza was back in Miss Violet's apartment, in plenty of time for their appointment. Miss Violet looked through the box of materials.

"You've done a wonderful job, Liza!" Miss Violet said delightedly. "Everything's neat, orderly, and in sequence. What fun I'll have looking over the story of my life when the scrapbook is finished. Of course, it won't really be finished until my life is over, will it? And my life isn't over yet. Not by a long shot!"

She set the box on her desk. "And now to the snapshots! We'll put them in sequence and keep a notebook detailing just who is in each picture. In case I should forget peoples' names and faces as time goes by. They say you tend to become more forgetful as you grow older. I personally believe that is a rumor entirely without foundation." As if in agreement, her small black cat pounced at her feet, then rubbed happily against her legs.

"That *is* a rumor," Liza assured her.

"We have two whole hours before Bella Vine comes," said Miss Violet. "There's plenty of time to sort through some of these pictures and label them." She pulled open the desk drawers. Liza could see that they were filled with snapshots. "We'll jot down in the notebook a number and description of each one," Miss Violet told her. "Just the way we'd planned before you went to Seattle. Later, at your leisure, you can arrange them chronologically."

Liza liked these projects with Miss Violet. She had learned a lot from them already.

They sat at a table and began to look at the snapshots. "This is my dear friend Annie, the one who has left me all the money." Miss Violet reached over and tapped Liza's notebook. "Write down 'Annie Banderly, London.'" She studied the picture, which showed an elderly woman with a crown of braids. "I believe this snapshot was taken in the fall of 1975."

Liza wrote in the notebook the number *1* and the name of the person and date. She copied the same information on the back of the picture.

"And this shows me with Helga, Jessie's wife. The picture was taken in front of their house, probably in 1974. Jessie and I lost touch after that. The next thing I knew he was dead."

Liza glanced at the picture. A younger Miss Violet stood next to an Amazon of a woman with a very large nose and chin.

Miss Violet reached in the desk drawer and pulled out another picture. "This is Sam Wooser," she said. "And there's Jessie. I don't think he meant to have his picture taken—he looks so surprised."

She peered at the picture intently. "This isn't a very good picture of Jessie, but it's the only one I have. I wrote to his wife after he died to tell her how much I treasure it."

She turned the snapshot over and thought for

a moment. "Sam's wife, Jackie, had a Polaroid camera. She took lots of pictures of Sam's last day at work. I was in Europe at the time, and she was thoughtful enough to leave several pictures in my mailbox. She knew how sorry I was to see Sam leave the Brillstone."

She peered again at the snapshot and chuckled. "The staff had given him that ridiculous big pocket watch. A nice wristwatch would have been so much more useful. Who wears pocket watches these days?" She handed the snapshot to Liza.

Liza studied it. She was curious to see what Jessie had looked like.

"I'm going to fix us a little snack," said Miss Violet, standing up. "Tea and cookies would taste just right. The water's already boiling." She set the cat on the floor and went out to the kitchen.

Liza continued to stare at the picture. Jessie was looking over his shoulder at the camera. Miss Violet was right: he did look surprised. His eyebrows were thick and dark, and so was his hair. He wore his hair long, covering his ears. He and Sam Wooser were both tall, about the same height.

Miss Violet returned with the tea and set the

tray between her and Liza. "Refreshments, my dear, have the name *refreshment* because they are meant to be refreshing." Her eyes twinkled.

She glanced at Liza, who was still studying the picture. "Yes, that was taken on Sam's retirement day. It's sad that all he had to show for his years at the Brillstone was a silly, ugly pocket watch pointing grandly to noon!" She started to pour the tea. "Mark down in the notebook the occasion—Sam's retirement. Now let me try to think of the date. That was such a busy time for me. I was in London, and then Paris, visiting dear friends." She set the teapot down and frowned. "May. Five years ago. That's close enough, I think, my dear."

Liza wrote on the back of the picture and entered the same words in the book: "Sam Wooser, retirement." Then she added the month and year. She hesitated a moment and wrote: "Jessie in background."

Liza and Miss Violet drank the tea and munched on the cookies while they worked.

Suddenly Miss Violet glanced at her watch. "Oh dear, how on earth did our time go so fast? Bella Vine will be arriving in a few minutes. And she instructed me to lie down and have empty thoughts before she came. How extraordinary! Who can do that, I wonder?"

Liza laughed as she returned the snapshots to the desk drawer and put the notebook on one of the shelves. She'd come back tomorrow to work on the project.

Miss Violet picked up the cat. "Bainbridge, can we have empty thoughts, do you think?" She rubbed his head. "I feel so tempted to give the money to the Cat's Meow. It's such a worthwhile cause. Stray cats have been one of my main concerns for many years. And do you know how I became interested in cats, Liza?"

She shook her head. "You've never told me, Miss Violet."

"Well, many years ago I came upon a poor waif of a kitten. She was all wet. She was starving and miserable. I took her home and nursed her back to health." She shook her head fondly. "We became fast friends, that cat and I. Our meeting came at a fortuitous time for me. I was lonely and at loose ends. Finding the stray kitten seemed to turn my fortune around."

"What was the cat's name?" asked Liza.

Miss Violet laughed. "Do you know, my dear, I have been trying for years to remember her name. And I simply can't. It's escaped me." She sighed. "Maybe it will come to me. Maybe we'll find a snapshot of her that will jog my memory."

She set the cat down. "Of course, I am sorely tempted to give my inheritance to help stray cats. But I must have an open mind. I don't know what I'll do."

Liza felt a quick stab of sympathy—and worry—for Miss Violet. Would Bella Vine sway Miss Violet during their meeting?

"I'm rather curious about today's session," Miss Violet said, as though reading Liza's mind. "We're to have a seance, I believe. I've never been in one. I wonder if I'll be good at it."

"You'll be great," Liza said, not feeling at all sure about Bella Vine's intentions. Would Bella Vine try to hypnotize Miss Violet? Would she pretend to summon Jessie's ghost?

"I must get ready, dear. I'm going to try to empty my fuddled head of thoughts before Bella Vine arrives. I'll just lie down in my room till she comes. You can let yourself out."

"Don't worry about a thing," Liza urged her.

Miss Violet smiled gratefully. She picked up the cat, turned to her bedroom, and closed the door.

Liza had straightened up everything and started toward the door when a sudden inspiration hit her. She would hide in the closet and listen to the seance. She could find out what Bella Vine was up to. Liza opened the apartment door, waited a few seconds, and then closed it again. Miss Violet would think she had left.

Liza hurried to the closet in the living room and sat on the floor, quietly pulling the door shut behind her. Then, afraid that she wouldn't be able to hear, she opened it just a crack.

After a few minutes, she decided that the worst place to be was in a closet—in the dark. But it was too late to change her mind. She shifted her position and waited silently.

Chapter Five

Hiding in the dark closet, Liza finally heard a loud rapping on Miss Violet's front door.

"Here I come!" called Miss Violet's voice from somewhere in the apartment. "My head is empty. Here I come!"

Liza was relieved that she could hear so clearly.

"This is a good day," announced Bella Vine in her soft voice when the door was opened. "You have clearly made an effort to rid your mind of the mundane, I can sense that."

"Is it that obvious?" Miss Violet asked.

"To me, only to me, our Miss Violet," Bella Vine crooned.

"Well, that's something, anyway," Miss Violet said with a sigh. "Shall we begin?"

There was a long silence. Liza wished she could see what was going on.

"Arrangements," Bella Vine murmured finally.

"Arrangements?" asked Miss Violet.

"Indeed," Bella Vine said. "We must let ourselves have as little contact with the mortal world as possible. May I?"

Liza heard Miss Violet's heavy drapes being pulled closed. The thin strip of light she'd been able to see under the door disappeared.

There was rustling. "The incense," Bella Vine said, and Liza heard a match being struck. In a moment the heady aroma of the incense found its way into her hiding place.

"One final consideration," came Bella Vine's soft voice.

"May we pull your little dining table into the center of the living room? It is best to be situated at an equal distance from the walls. Physical confinement makes it difficult to cross the barrier into the spiritual world."

"Certainly," Miss Violet agreed.

Liza heard some scraping and thudding, and then suddenly realized how much closer the voices were to her.

"Two chairs and then we're ready," Bella Vine said.

There were two more thuds and a squeaking sound. Liza guessed that Bella Vine and Miss Violet had seated themselves at the small table.

"It certainly is rather dark in here, isn't it?" Miss Violet asked. "For daytime, I mean."

"Indeed," Bella Vine whispered. "A candle now, to cast mortal shadows compatible with spirit shadows."

"Goodness!" said Miss Violet.

Liza quietly tried to shift her position in the closet. As she leaned to one side, she peeked out the crack in the door. She was shocked to discover that she could see the table, Bella Vine's face, Miss Violet's back, and a lighted candle. With painstaking caution, she moved onto her stomach and leaned on her elbows. She put her face against the crack in the door. The living room, except for the area illuminated by the flickering candle, looked as dark to her as her hiding place. The shadows that waved across Bella Vine's face changed her appearance from one second to the next. First her eyes seemed to shine, then they looked like deep caverns. Liza shivered.

"Hands must be held to make the circuit

complete," murmured Bella Vine. "Our energy fuses together and sends up an electrical pulse, or beat, if you will. The pulse, the charge, will contact another pulse from another energy plane. Let us hope that we will be able to contact a suitable plane together."

"Interesting," exclaimed Miss Violet. "All that just from holding hands? My, my."

"We must speak in hushed tones, our Miss Violet," said Bella Vine. "We cannot risk frightening off the nearly inaudible voices from beyond."

"Indeed," Miss Violet whispered.

Liza wished she could see Miss Violet's face. Was Miss Violet taking the seance seriously? Would Bella Vine make her believe in ghosts? Liza stared at Bella Vine's face. It was partly obscured by her thick, dark hair and the dark shadows that flickered across it.

For a long moment all Liza heard was deep breathing. Then Bella Vine broke the near silence. "I am aware . . . of a pulse."

Her husky, soft voice sent prickles all along Liza's scalp and back.

Surely there was really nothing to this seance. Yet for the first time Liza felt uncertain. She was unable to take her eyes off the spiritualist's calm, serene face. She found herself waiting eagerly to hear Bella Vine's strange voice again.

Were she and Miss Violet being hypnotized?

Bella Vine broke the silence once again. "It is clear, it is here," came her strange, hoarse whisper. She repeated the chant softly. "It is clear, it is here."

The candle's shadows danced furiously around the room, seeming to change the shapes of the furniture and of Bella and Miss Violet.

Liza blinked her eyes, trying to concentrate. Surely Bella Vine was only attempting to trick Miss Violet into believing in the spirit world. Or was she?

Would Bella Vine pretend to talk to Jessie?

She spoke again. "We are receiving your energy. We are aware of your astral presence."

Liza suddenly felt cold. Who was Bella Vine speaking to, anyway?

"I would like a sign. A sign . . . a sign . . ." Bella Vine's voice trailed off.

The candle grew dimmer.

And then a loud sound broke the silence.

Liza swallowed, the hair on the back of her neck standing on end.

A voice, loud and deep, spoke slowly: "Aunt Violet, I am here."

Liza heard Miss Violet suck in her breath and mutter, "Good gracious me, for heaven's sake!"

Liza wouldn't have believed in that strange voice if she hadn't heard it herself. Could Bella Vine talk like that? Could she make her voice sound so much like a man's?

Was there someone else—Jessie?—in the room?

Liza shook her head. She knew better than to believe that it was really Jessie speaking. That was impossible. Then why did her heart race and her flesh crawl?

The voice spoke again: "Omen. Omen." The words were repeated over and over in a loud, deep monotone. And then the voice began to change. It grew softer and softer. But it was still a man's voice.

Finally it stopped.

Bella Vine's soft, melodic voice took over. "Senalda," she said. "Senalda. Senalda."

Miss Violet gave another loud gasp. "Senalda! My first cat!" she cried. "How on earth...?"

Bella Vine spoke again. "There is more, from another energy pocket. I must—"

"No more," Miss Violet said abruptly. "Enough is enough."

Liza felt limp. Hearing the normal tone of Miss Violet's voice had snapped her back to reality.

"Do forgive me, dear," Miss Violet said. "I must admit I was fascinated with this show, almost alarmed. You certainly have a talent, dear. One thing is for sure: Jessie wouldn't come all the way back just to see me, heaven knows. And, quite frankly, my money wouldn't do him any good where he is."

Miss Violet sighed. "That's all water under the bridge, as they say. But what truly interests me is that you knew the name of my first cat, Senalda. You have your ways with the spirit world, dear, I'm quite sure. More important, you made something click in my mind, that's what you did, and for your help I am grateful."

Liza strained her eyes in the darkness and peered at Bella Vine's face. Although it was covered in shadows, Liza thought she could detect resentment and confusion. "I must get some light in here, I must!" Miss Violet announced.

She opened the heavy draperies, and bright light flooded the living room.

Miss Violet came back to the table and sat down. Liza saw that Bella Vine had extinguished the candle and the incense. Her arms were folded across her thick body.

"I was so startled when you said *Senalda*," Miss Violet began. "And the omen business surprised me, as well. That's what the name *Senalda* means in Spanish—omen. I always thought my first cat was a good omen for me." She paused, and Bella Vine shifted her weight on her chair. Liza heard the chair squeak.

Miss Violet continued. "I was jarred with that 'Aunt Violet, I am here' bit, I admit. But that sort of thing just doesn't sit right with me. It's not me at all, if you see what I mean. Many other people must go along with your seances, dear, otherwise you wouldn't have much business, you spiritualists. But you must understand that I just don't believe that Jessie would be calling to me from somewhere in the Great Beyond."

Bella Vine was silent.

"Well," Miss Violet said cheerfully, "you did make something click for me. I've made up my mind. Suddenly and with conviction, I know what I'm going to do with my money. And I know that my decision is right. And you helped me decide—admittedly in a strange way, but you helped."

Liza held her breath. What was Miss Violet going to do?

"I've decided to hand over my check to Phyllis Baker for the Cat's Meow," Miss Violet said firmly. "Coincidence or spiritual readings aside, I feel that I'm right. Hearing my cat Senalda's name again was a good omen."

Liza could hardly contain herself. Miss Violet was going to give her money to the cat shelter— not the Seekers. She stared at Bella Vine. The woman's face was unreadable.

"If you must, you must," she said after a moment. "I had hoped to reach another astral plane. Perhaps another time?"

"I think not," Miss Violet said kindly. "Although I wouldn't mind visiting with you anytime you choose. Quite frankly, I don't believe I'm cut out for seances."

And neither am I, Liza thought.

"Now that I've made up my mind, I wish I could act immediately," said Miss Violet, her voice a notch higher with concern. "If only I could hand the check to Phyllis Baker right now. But I feel good, having made up my mind. Yes, I feel quite lighthearted," Miss Violet said with a sigh. "Did you ever meet Phyllis Baker? A lovely woman. She'll be pleased about my decision."

"We did cross paths, our Miss Violet," Bella Vine said. "I was leaving and she was coming, or it was the other way around. You have visited with many people recently. I truly hope that you have made the right decision."

"Oh, I have, I have," Miss Violet said. "You know, I hate to cut short this session, but rather suddenly I feel tired and think I'll lie down. Let yourself out. I'll move the table later. And thank you again for helping me make a decision."

Miss Violet headed toward her bedroom. As Liza watched, she planned her exit. She would wait until Bella Vine had left, and then she would quietly let herself out the front door. She couldn't wait to tell Logan about Miss Violet's decision.

Liza heard the rustling of Bella Vine's clothing and a sudden click. The click must have been the clasp on Bella Vine's large pillowcaselike bag, Liza thought. Then she heard the apartment door open and close.

She decided to give herself three or four minutes before leaving, to be safe. She was surprised when just a couple of minutes had passed and she heard a steady, soft snoring from the direction of Miss Violet's bedroom. Liza could leave now. She began to stand up when suddenly she heard the apartment door opening. Startled, she pulled the closet door shut and held her breath. Someone was moving around in the living room. The person paused. Liza heard a desk drawer being pulled open. Then another.

The person in the living room began to softly whistle "Mary Had a Little Lamb."

Liza felt goosebumps rise all over her. If only she had left the door cracked open so that she could see.

Was there really someone out there? Or was it—? No, there weren't such things as ghosts.

Could someone be looking through the pictures in the desk drawers?

Liza waited, her heart pounding. The soft whistling of "Mary Had a Little Lamb"—or "Violet Had a Little Cat"—continued.

She heard a desk drawer being closed, and then footsteps again.

The apartment door opened and closed firmly. The intruder had left.

Liza straightened up and opened the closet door. The bright light made her blink, and she looked around. The living room was empty. Who had been in here, only seconds before?

Whoever had come had been looking for something in the desk. The only things in the desk drawers were snapshots, all filed and numbered. Someone had wanted a photograph. And whoever it was must have found it.

Liza wasted no time. She opened the desk drawers and thumbed through the consecutively numbered pictures. All were there except for number 3. Her heart pounded faster as she pulled out the master list of the numbered photographs. She ran her thumb down to the third entry and read her handwriting: "Sam Wooser, retirement. Jessie in background."

Liza shook her head, not understanding. She felt a wave of confusion, mixed with fear. Who would have known about the picture of Sam Wooser? Who would have wanted it? Sam? But why?

She quietly returned the master list to the shelf and hurried out of Miss Violet's apartment. Logan would be home from work by now. She had to talk to him.

Chapter Six

Logan was glad when work was over. He had worried all day about Miss Violet. He couldn't shake the feeling that Bella Vine and Sam Wooser were trying to deceive her in some way.

He drove home slowly and carefully through the dense fog. It still hung like a thick, gray blanket over the city.

Logan breathed a sigh of relief when his car was finally safely parked in the Brillstone garage. He hurried to the elevator.

As he stepped out onto his floor, he saw a heavy, dark figure leaving Miss Violet's apartment. It was Bella Vine! Her long layers of clothes spun around her as she ran in the opposite direction down the corridor, her enormous soft bag swinging.

She was running toward the door to the stairs. Logan hesitated. What was she up to, anyway? Was she planning to walk all the way downstairs?

He headed down the corridor after her. The door to the stairway swung softly shut as he reached it. He waited a few seconds, then cautiously opened it and listened. Bella Vine was going up the stairs, not down them. Logan hugged the wall of the stairwell as he started up, too.

Bella Vine kept climbing beyond the eighth floor. Suddenly Logan realized that she was going to the roof. He stopped when she paused to catch her breath.

Then he heard the heavy creaking of the big iron door to the roof and felt cold, damp air against his face.

He ran up the rest of the stairs two at a time and reached the iron door just as it swung shut. He opened it slowly and peered out. Dark shapes of heating vents and chimneys hovered mysteriously in the gray mist. There was no trace of Bella Vine.

Logan strained to hear a tell-tale sound but could detect only the wind, whistling shrilly. Now and then it made a slapping sound as it beat at loose strips of tarpaper.

He inched his way across the rooftop and nearly bumped into something large and dark. He felt it with outstretched palms and realized it must be some kind of shack. He had heard Louie say that the roof was being repaired. Maybe the shack had been put up by the roofing company.

Taking a deep breath, Logan peered inside, prepared to confront Bella Vine, face to face.

The shack was empty.

He frowned, turned, and peered again into the thick fog. Where had Bella Vine disappeared to?

Suddenly Logan was aware of a slow creaking. The iron door behind him was being opened. He whirled around. A tall black figure emerged from the stairwell. It seemed to float through the fog toward Logan. And then distinctly in the wind, Logan heard the whistled tune he had heard twice before: "Mary Had a Little Lamb."

He pressed himself against the side of the

shack as the dark figure brushed by him and disappeared around the other side.

And then, in a low voice, Logan heard the words, "Is that you, Jessie?"

Logan stood rooted to the spot. He heard snatches of words—a man's voice, a woman's voice. But the shrill wind kept him from hearing what they were saying.

Suddenly the black figure hurried past Logan, unaware of his presence. Logan heard the iron door to the stairwell being pulled open. The dark figure disappeared.

Logan hesitated. Should he stay and confront the person—Bella Vine?—who was still on the roof? Or should he follow the black figure?

He made a decision. He was going to settle this mystery once and for all. He'd find out who was pretending to be Jessie's ghost.

He started through the door. Inside the stairwell, he heard the sound of a landing door being pulled open. Logan waited for a moment, then hurried down the stairs and pulled open the same door.

A man was stepping onto one of the elevators. He was dressed in a black raincoat and a black rain hat.

Logan raced to the other elevator, pressed the button, and waited with desperate impatience for it to come. He watched as the indicator on the other elevator swept around. By the time Logan's elevator had come for him, the other elevator had already reached the ground.

It seemed endless minutes before Logan reached the first floor.

Quickly he ran through the lobby. It was empty except for a delivery man Logan had seen many times before.

Where had the strange figure disappeared to?

Logan pushed through the revolving doors, and the fog suddenly enveloped him. He ran down the circular driveway. The street lights, yellow and dim, glowed eerily. There was little automobile traffic, but several buses made their careful way along the street. As the leading bus stopped at the corner, Logan saw with relief that he hadn't lost the man, after all. There he was, just stepping into the front bus.

Logan ran to catch up, but the light changed. The bus switched gears and moved on.

He ran on the sidewalk, trying to look into the bus. There were several passengers, and at first Logan couldn't distinguish one from the other.

Then he saw the man in the black raincoat and hat move to the back of the bus.

Logan looked behind him. Half a block away, he could just make out the headlights of the second bus. He made a quick decision. He ran back to the bus stop and climbed on the bus when it stopped for him. He put his money in the fare box and peered through the windshield at the bus ahead.

"Durn fog," the driver said, leaning forward on the huge steering wheel. "Can't see why people want to be outside in this stuff. Soup is to eat, not to drive in."

Logan smiled politely and then asked, "Mind if I stand up here?"

"Suit yourself." The driver shrugged. Logan tried to keep the first bus in view. Each time it came to a stop, Logan watched with mounting anticipation as the passengers dismounted. So far so good. The man in the black raincoat hadn't got off. He still had to be on the bus.

In a few moments Logan saw the first bus turn right and head toward the west side of town. With relief, he watched his bus driver turn in the same direction.

The neighborhood began to change. Now

there were no more busy, brightly lighted storefronts, and there were fewer traffic lights. Occasional stop signs halted the steady progress of the buses. The road became narrower. Logan could pick out tall, shabby buildings through the fog and dark.

At last the bus ahead stopped, and Logan saw the dark, hatted figure get off.

"Mine's the next stop," Logan told the driver. He stepped down to the street. Although he was just yards from the strange figure, it was impossible to see him clearly. In the fog, Logan could tell only that he was in a hurry.

Logan followed, the gravel crunching beneath his feet. But the man did not seem to hear.

Suddenly the man turned to enter a dimly lighted storefront.

Logan stopped and studied the building. It looked grimy in the fog.

So this was where the man had come! Logan stepped closer to the window. He could pick out a few dim light bulbs inside.

Suddenly Logan's breath caught in his throat. Dozens of arms, legs, heads, and torsos hung from the high ceiling of the store. They were parts of mannequins—dummies!

Logan stepped back and glanced at the storefront again. On the door, in chipped, white paint, was spelled out: "Majestic Theatrical Supplies. Props. Mannequins Made to Order."

Logan looked up and down the street. It was obvious that most of the other stores in the neighborhood had already closed. He looked at the hours posted on the door of the supplies shop: 12 to 5. It was after five now. Still, Logan was positive the man had come here.

He peered inside again and saw a movement.

Had one of the mannequins changed position? But mannequins don't move, Logan reminded himself.

There. He saw something move again, behind a low counter.

Gathering courage, Logan turned the handle on the door. It was unlocked. The door swung open on a rusted, squeaky hinge.

As Logan approached the counter, a musty odor filled his nostrils. His shoulder caught on something, and a mannequin swung around.

"Hello?" Logan called. There was no one behind the counter now. Logan's voice seemed to catch on the high ceiling and bounce back at him. He could almost believe that if he turned around, each and every mannequin would be turning to answer his call.

"Is anyone here?" Logan tried again. He stared in amazement. He'd never seen a place like this before. He looked up to a small, high balcony at the far side of the store. An ornate, wrought-iron staircase led up to it.

A man and a woman sat at a small table on the balcony. Dressed beautifully, they each held a glass. They were perfectly still. They must be part of a display, Logan thought.

Suddenly he was aware that a man was standing behind the counter—a man who hadn't been there a moment ago.

He was small and pale and almost hairless. His eyes were set very close together. He stared at Logan without expression.

"A man came in here," Logan began. "Can you tell me where he is?"

The small man continued to stare at Logan. He said nothing. His long, bony fingers were spread out on the counter.

Logan made another effort. "Someone just came in here."

The man's face remained still except for a small tic under his right eye.

"I know he came in here," Logan insisted, feeling uneasy.

The small man still did not speak.

From a distance, came the muffled whistling of "Mary Had a Little Lamb."

Logan blinked, looking around him. Nothing alive greeted him: only the grotesque limbs and torsos and heads that hung silently.

He looked back at the man, who seemed not to hear the whistling.

Where was the sound coming from?

And then Logan spotted a door at the back of the shop. He glanced at the small, pale man, then back at the door, suddenly realizing that he would not be able to find out what was behind it. Not with this strangely silent man standing guard.

As if the man were reading Logan's mind, he stretched his arm in the direction of the front door and gestured with a long, bony finger for Logan to leave.

Logan sighed inwardly, confused and frustrated. Who was this person who wouldn't speak to him? The man obviously wanted Logan to leave. Was he hiding Sam? Jessie's ghost? Logan knew someone was behind that door. He could still hear the faint whistling.

He had no choice. He would have to leave.

On his way out the door, he turned back to look over his shoulder. The small, pale man was walking toward him.

Once outside, Logan heard the click of a lock and saw the lights go off one by one.

He glanced back at the store as he hurried to the bus stop. He could see only darkness and fog. It was as though a giant, muddy thumb had squashed the shop's existence.

When he finally reached the Brillstone Apartments, he was damp and cold and hungry. But he had to tell Liza everything. He knocked at her door.

Chapter Seven

I thought you'd never get home from work," said Liza as she opened the door to Logan.

Logan came in and sank down in Webb's chair. When he had caught his breath, he told Liza about following Bella Vine to the roof and chasing "Jessie" through the fog to the odd shop. And then Liza told her story of the seance—of the strange voice that said "Aunt Violet, I am here"— and of the person who had come into Miss Violet's afterwards to steal the snapshot of Sam and Jessie.

"Why would someone steal the picture?" wondered Logan.

"Why any of it?" asked Liza, pacing.

She wheeled around and sat down on the couch. "Let's get the time sequence straight," she suggested. "You must have seen Bella Vine when she was leaving Miss Violet's after the seance."

"And right after that, someone came into Miss Violet's and stole the snapshot of Sam Wooser and Jessie," said Logan.

"I'll bet Bella Vine unlocked the apartment door as she left," Liza said suddenly. "To let someone in."

"And then the person must have come up to the roof to meet her," Logan concluded. He shivered, remembering the eerie whistling and the snatches of conversation: "Is that you, Jessie?"

"Jessie's dead, and I refuse to believe in ghosts," said Liza. "The person on the roof must have been the person who's pretending to be Jessie's ghost. And the strange voice in the seance must have been Bella Vine."

"I think it was Sam Wooser on the roof," said Logan. "I saw him talking to Bella Vine yesterday. I think they're in cahoots, trying to convince Miss Violet that Bella Vine has established contact with the spirit world—and Jessie."

"It could be Sam Wooser," said Liza. "Or it

might be someone we've never heard of. Someone who's working with Bella Vine."

"Sam Wooser just came back to the Brillstone after years away," Logan said. "Why? It seems obvious. He came because he heard about Miss Violet's inheritance."

"Maybe," admitted Liza. "But why would he want that picture? Why would *anyone* want it?"

"I don't know," said Logan. "But there's got to be a good reason. Maybe he wanted to show Bella Vine what Jessie looked like."

Logan started to pace. "And what *did* he look like?" he asked.

Liza tried to remember the snapshot. "He had dark, thick eyebrows and hair. He wore his hair long—down over his ears."

"How tall was he?" asked Logan.

"About the same height as Sam Wooser. Why?"

Logan turned around. "Because maybe Sam Wooser wanted that picture so he could fix himself up to look like Jessie. They're about the same height. If Sam had some bushy eyebrows and a wig—"

Liza swallowed. "I think you've got it, Logan," she said. "Sam wanted to make himself up to look just like Jessie so that he could appear at one of Bella Vine's seances and convince Miss Violet that he was talking to her from the grave. In the seance today Miss Violet heard Jessie's voice. In the next one, she would have *seen* Jessie. Sam wanted her to leave the inheritance to Bella Vine and the Seekers."

"Right," said Logan. "He knew Jessie, so he'd have known about the whistle and all sorts of other things, like the name *Senalda.*"

Logan drummed his fingers on the table and looked at Liza. "Hey, we're right, and you know what? Suddenly I'm starved. What's for dinner, anyway?"

"Mrs. Merkle's marvelous homemade stew," Liza said. "Webb and Jenny are invited out for dinner and a concert. We're on our own."

"I'll set the table," said Logan. He got the silverware out of the drawer while Liza poured the stew into a serving bowl.

"Miss Violet told Bella Vine that she planned to give the money to the Cat's Meow," she said. "But I almost wish she hadn't said that in front of her. What if Bella Vine tries to change Miss Violet's mind?"

Logan paused in the middle of setting the

table. "That's possible," he said. "Bella Vine and Sam have a meeting on the roof. He dashes off to some strange neighborhood. I lose him. Meanwhile, what does Bella Vine do, up there on the roof?"

"Let's try to picture the whole thing," suggested Liza. "Sam comes into Miss Violet's apartment. I'm hiding in the closet. He gets the picture he's been looking for. He and Bella Vine have planned all this ahead. She left Miss Violet's door unlocked after the seance so that he could get in and look for the picture."

Logan nodded. "And they also planned to meet on the roof afterwards, where no one would see them. I wonder what they talked about."

"Probably about the seance," said Liza, "and the fact that Miss Violet had decided to leave her money to the cat shelter, after all—not the Seekers."

"Yes," agreed Logan. "So there was nothing more they could do. It was too late to try to dress Sam up like Jessie to fool Miss Violet."

Liza frowned. "Unless they still think they can try to change her mind," she said. "I think we should warn Miss Violet."

Liza went quickly over to the telephone. She

dialed Miss Violet's number and waited impatiently. "She's not home. We'll have to try later," she said.

Logan and Liza sat down at the kitchen table. Logan passed the dish of stew.

They gulped their food.

After a while, Liza got up and nervously dialed Miss Violet's number again. But there was still no answer.

"Maybe something's wrong," she said. "Maybe we should go check her apartment."

Logan nodded.

The two of them let themselves out of Liza's apartment and ran down the back stairs to the seventh floor.

When they got to Miss Violet's, Liza knocked.

All was quiet.

Where had Miss Violet gone?

"Maybe it's silly to worry," said Liza. "Miss Violet often visits her friends. She probably just decided to go away for a day or so, that's all."

"I guess you're right." Logan knocked at Miss Violet's door one more time. "We don't have to break down the door or call the Marines or the police or anything."

But after he had said goodnight to Liza, he

came back and tried Miss Violet's apartment once more. There was still no answer.

Logan jumped awake in a cold sweat. He'd been having a dream, that was it. About Miss Violet. She was in trouble, real trouble. And Logan was powerless to help her. But the dream faded, leaving him with a sense of uneasiness.

He turned over and as he did so, thought of the early morning a hundred years ago when he had wakened to the sound of the whistling. So much had happened since then. It was hard to believe he had heard the mysterious whistling just the day before yesterday.

He turned over again restlessly and glanced at his clock. It was too early to get up. Yet he was wide awake. His thoughts turned again to Miss Violet and the fact that she had disappeared.

There were a dozen easy explanations. She'd gone to visit a friend. That was it. She certainly had a lot of friends. No relatives, but friends. He remembered that Jessie had been her only living relative. And now there were none.

He turned again. Where had she gone? He thought of Bella Vine and Sam—it must have been Sam—up on the roof. What had they been talking about? They must have been unhappy that Miss Violet had decided to give her money to the cat shelter. And they could do nothing about it.

Logan sat up. Maybe there *was* something they could do. Maybe Miss Violet hadn't given the check to Phyllis Baker. Maybe Sam Wooser and Bella Vine could force her to sign over a check to them. Maybe Miss Violet was being held against her will. Maybe she had been kidnapped!

Logan put his feet on the floor. Bella Vine and Sam had met on the roof yesterday afternoon. Bella Vine had known then that the money was going to go to the cat shelter. *Going* to go—but had not gone. Maybe she and Sam Wooser had planned the kidnapping then. Sam had taken a bus to the strange little shop. Bella Vine had stayed on the roof—for how long? Had Sam left, knowing Logan would follow him? Had Sam led Logan on a wild-goose chase to get him out of the way—so that Bella Vine could go down to Miss Violet's apartment? And then had Bella Vine kidnapped her? Was Bella Vine holding Miss Violet somewhere until she signed the check?

Logan stood up. He ran his hands through his unruly hair. He had to talk to Liza. He reached for the telephone. It was pretty early for her, but this was too important to wait.

Her sleepy voice answered on the third ring.

"Liza, I've thought of something important. I'll come up in five. Okay?"

"Five what?" she asked sleepily. "Is it morning?"

"It will be by the time I get there," Logan told her and hung up.

Quickly he showered and dressed. In five minutes he was running up the stairs.

An envelope was propped against Liza's door. He leaned over and picked it up. Miss Violet's familiar handwriting was sprawled across the front of the envelope: "To Liza."

Logan held the envelope up to the light. Could it contain a ransom note?

He tapped on the door.

Liza, sleepy-eyed, opened it at once.

Logan handed her the note. "I've been worrying about Miss Violet, thinking maybe Bella Vine and Sam have kidnapped her."

Liza stared at him, then at the envelope. Logan closed the door behind him as Liza tore open the envelope. A key was enclosed with the note. Logan read over her shoulder:

Liza, my dear,

What a relief! Phyllis Baker stopped in not long after I had my seance with Bella Vine. I was able to give her the check for the cat shelter. Needless to say, she is most happy about it, and so am I.

With that off my mind, I've decided to go on a little spree and am taking the train tonight to visit an old friend who loves cats as I do. Of course, I am taking Bainbridge with me.

Two favors, dear Liza. One, I have written several letters and although I have put them in their envelopes with the names of the appropriate parties, I must ask you to add the right addresses and stamp the envelopes. Here is my key so that you can do so this morning. Two, will you please call me at the telephone number below? I must give you two of the addresses on the telephone. I don't have them now, but I will obtain them from a friend. Be sure to call, as those two letters are quite important.

Thank you.
Your friend,
Violet Cunningham

P.S. My first cat's name was Senalda!

Logan tossed his keys in the air with relief. "Then she's all right," he said with a sigh. "I really had talked myself into the idea that Bella Vine and Sam had done something to her."

"There's nothing they can do," said Liza with satisfaction. "Phyllis has the check now."

"But still, Bella Vine and Sam shouldn't be able to get away with their plot about the Seekers," complained Logan.

Liza frowned. "Well, let's talk everything over with Dad and Jenny." She grinned at Logan. "Like all normal people, Dad's sound asleep, and I expect Jenny is, too."

Logan grinned back. "Like all normal people, I'm starved. I'll fry bacon if you scramble eggs."

"Fair enough," said Liza. "I'll take a shower while the bacon is baconing. Then we can run down to Miss Violet's."

The telephone rang. "Well, someone's awake, anyway," said Liza, picking up the receiver.

Logan walked out to the kitchen. In a moment, Liza stuck her head in the door. "That was Louie," she said. "He wanted to make sure I'd found that letter from Miss Violet. She left it on his desk last night and asked him to deliver it this morning."

Logan whistled as he opened the refrigerator and poured himself a tall glass of orange juice. Then out of the corner of his eye, he noticed the roses on the counter. Logan stopped whistling. The card was propped up against the vase: "I miss you already. Dan."

Chapter Eight

As soon as Liza and Logan had finished breakfast, they started downstairs to Miss Violet's.

"I sure wish I had known last night that everything was all right," Liza said as she and Logan approached Miss Violet's apartment. "It would have saved me a nasty dream or two."

"And me, too," Logan said. Tonight he planned to dream that Dan was swallowed by a giant steelhead. That would be a good dream.

Liza pulled Miss Violet's key out of her pocket and opened the door. As she and Logan stepped into the living room, she was surprised to see how dark it was—as dark as it had been yesterday during Bella Vine's seance. The heavy draperies were again pulled closed.

Liza started to put her hand to the wall switch but suddenly pulled back. She stiffened, clutching Logan's arm.

A loud, thudding noise came from somewhere

inside the apartment. It sounded as if a piece of furniture was being pulled across the floor.

There was someone in the dark apartment. Logan stepped farther into the living room. The thudding sound had stopped, and now another sound replaced it—a soft, sliding noise.

The sound came from behind the closed door to Miss Violet's bedroom.

Liza looked over at Logan and knew that he, too, was waiting tensely for another sound, a sound familiar to them both—the whistled tune of "Mary Had a Little Lamb."

But no whistle came—only more soft thuds. Then, as Logan and Liza stood staring in the direction of the bedroom, a faint crack of light appeared. It widened slowly.

Liza sucked in her breath as a pale, bent form passed through the doorway.

It was hard to see in the dark living room, and Logan quickly made a decision. He pivoted and flicked on the wall switch.

Light flooded the living room, and a man in white coveralls jumped back. Something he had been holding in his hands fell to the floor.

He looked up. In the light he didn't seem pale, at all.

Logan and Liza stared. "It's you! You're Sam!" Logan blurted out.

"You've been plotting against Miss Violet all along," Liza said angrily. "You were working with Bella Vine and trying to make Miss Violet think that Jessie was talking to her from the grave. Just so you could get her money."

The man bent down to pick up what he had dropped. It was a small, delicately carved box.

"You're even stealing Miss Violet's favorite jewelry box!" Liza cried.

The man stared hard at Logan and Liza. He seemed bewildered. "I wonder, now, what you two are talking about. What's this story about Jessie's spirit? And Bella Vine? And Miss Violet's money?" He shook his head. "You've got the wrong person, kids."

He held up the carved box. "I'm not stealing this, if that's what's bothering you. Miss Violet knows I'm good with my hands. She asked if I'd repair the hinges while she's gone. They'd come loose. I took out all of her jewelry and put it at the back of her closet shelf in her bedroom. You can see for yourselves."

It would be easy enough to prove, Logan thought—or disprove.

"Not that it's any of your business what I'm doing here," Sam went on. "For all I know, you were planning to steal the box yourselves. You seem to know what Miss Violet keeps in it. Maybe you have some explaining to do, too."

He eyed Logan and Liza carefully. "But look, kids. I don't want an argument any more than you do. Please tell me what you meant when you said something about Jessie rising from the grave. And what's this about Miss Violet's money?" He looked at Liza. "Is someone really trying to play a trick on Miss Violet?"

"As if you didn't know," Liza said coldly.

Sam frowned and set the carved box down on the small table next to Miss Violet's chair. "You two really do believe something's wrong and that I'm behind it. You're sincere, but you're mistaken."

Mistaken? Logan and Liza glanced at each other. Of course Sam was behind it.

"We have proof," Liza said, raising her chin defiantly. "I—" She hesitated a second. "I saw you. I was in the closet when you came in and stole the picture."

Logan added, "And I saw you talking to Bella Vine in the hallway and up on the roof. Then I followed you on the bus to the other side of town."

Sam ran a hand through his graying hair. "First of all, I never came in here to steal a picture." He studied Liza intently. "I might ask what *you* were doing hiding in the closet, but that can wait. Second of all, I haven't been on a bus in years. I've got my own car." Logan and Liza exchanged glances.

"You may be right about one thing, though," Sam went on. "I did run into an oddly dressed woman in the hall yesterday, but quite by accident. So please, now, the story. I want all of it. It sounds to me as if something around here is very wrong. I want to know what has been going on at the Brillstone."

Logan hesitated. Why should they explain things to Sam? After all, it was Sam who was in the wrong, not Logan and Liza.

Liza spoke up. "It sounds to me as if you're trying to fool us just the way you were trying to con Miss Violet. Of course, you know that it's too late to trick her now. She has already made out a check to the animal shelter—not the Seekers. So everything you did was for nothing." She added the last with defiance.

Sam didn't seem surprised, Logan noticed. Or disappointed or shocked. Maybe he thought he and Bella Vine still had a chance.

"In fact, Phyllis Baker already has the check for the Cat's Meow shelter," Logan stated. "There's nothing you can do now."

"Nor would I want to," Sam said, confused. "Miss Violet should follow her own wishes, shouldn't she? I don't understand what all the fuss is about—especially why you keep talking about Jessie and this Bella somebody."

Logan and Liza looked at each other. Could they be mistaken? Was Sam as innocent as he appeared? If he was, then who was pretending to be Jessie?

Logan went into Miss Violet's bedroom. He found her jewelry at the back of her closet shelf, where Sam said he had put it.

"You were telling the truth," Logan said as he came back into the living room. "I'm sorry we didn't believe you."

Sam waved his hand impatiently. "Look, if there's something that might put Miss Violet in danger, you must talk to me about it. If she needs help, we must act fast." His voice had become stern.

Logan glanced at Liza. She nodded, and Logan took a deep breath. "I'll tell you everything we know," he said finally. "First of all, sometime after midnight the day before yesterday, someone who must have had a key to my apartment came in and opened and closed the desk drawers. He—or she—was whistling 'Mary Had a Little Lamb.' Miss Violet told me later her dead nephew Jessie always whistled that tune. It was a nervous habit of his. Then I heard the same whistle late in the afternoon. I was in the elevator, but the lights were off, so I couldn't see who it was."

Sam nodded, his forehead creased with concentration. "Go on."

"Shortly after that, around five-thirty, someone came back to my apartment," Logan continued. "I saw the door closing, but when I looked there was no one in the corridor. I—"

"Wait," Sam said, putting up his hand. "You said you saw your door close around five-thirty? That last intruder must have been me."

Logan nodded, staring at Sam.

"Miss Violet had asked me to come over," Sam went on. "She'd said she'd leave her door unlocked. When I worked here several years ago, she lived across the hall, where you live now. The door to your apartment was unlocked, so I assumed I had the right apartment—until I opened the door."

Logan frowned. He'd had a lot on his mind, he remembered. Maybe he *had* left the door unlocked.

Sam continued, "So I just closed the door. Miss Violet was waiting for me and drew me right into her apartment. That's why you didn't see me."

Logan glanced over at Liza. He could tell that she was thinking the same thing he was. Miss Violet had lived in his apartment before he and Jenny did. That might explain a lot of things.

Logan cleared his throat. "Yesterday, when Bella Vine—"

"I'm sorry to keep interrupting you," Sam said, "but who is this Bella Vine?"

"Miss Violet's spiritualist," Liza said. "A dangerous one, we think."

Sam nodded.

"Anyway," Logan explained, "Bella Vine was having a seance with Miss Violet, and Liza hid in the closet to find out if Bella Vine was going to do anything odd, like hypnotize Miss Violet, to get her to give the Seekers her money. The Seekers is a group Bella Vine says she represents."

"The seance was spooky," Liza admitted, turning and sitting on the small chair at the desk. "I heard a voice—it must have been Bella Vine pretending to be Jessie—that said, 'Aunt Violet, I am here.'"

"So that's what you were doing in the closet!" Sam said.

Liza glanced up at him. He looked at her kindly. "After Bella Vine left," Liza went on, "I waited a minute or two, just to be on the safe side before leaving. But someone came in. Whoever it was whistled 'Mary Had a Little Lamb' and went through the drawers in this living-room desk."

"What for, I wonder?" Sam asked.

"For a picture, a certain picture," Liza said.

"Oh yes, that's right," Sam said. "You did accuse me of stealing a picture while you hid in the closet."

Liza smiled and then went on. "The person found the picture and took it. I know which one, because Miss Violet and I had started a master list describing each photograph she has. The thief took number *3.*" Liza paused and studied Sam again. "It was a picture of you with Jessie in the background."

Sam rubbed the cleft of his chin. "Of me and Jessie? That doesn't make sense. At least not to me. What else was in the picture?"

"Just you and Jessie," Liza said. "You were holding up a big pocket watch and smiling. Jessie was there, in the background."

"That's odd," Sam said, still rubbing his chin. "I can't remember a time when Jessie and I were together."

"Miss Violet couldn't remember the exact date the picture was taken," Liza said. "But she was pretty sure it was sometime in May, five years ago."

"Oh, wait a minute," Sam said. "I do remember." He moved over to the couch and sat down. "I remember the date very well. It was my retirement day. My wife and I had really looked forward to it. We flew to Arizona that very afternoon."

"What about the watch?" Logan asked, "And Jessie?"

"Well, the watch was a gift from the staff," Sam said. "And Jessie had come to see Miss Violet. But she was out of town. He didn't come to the Brillstone often, just when he was running a little short of cash. Miss Violet was always very generous with him. Too generous, perhaps."

Liza picked up a pen and absently tapped it on the edge of the desk. "I thought it was you who had stolen the picture so you could make yourself look like Jessie," Liza admitted.

"Why would I ever want to look like Jessie?" Sam wondered aloud.

"To convince Miss Violet that Jessie's spirit was alive and well and in need of cash," Logan explained sarcastically.

"What a plot!" Sam said.

"But if it wasn't you who stole the picture, who was it?" Liza demanded. "And who could possibly want the photograph?"

"I can't begin to guess," Sam said, his forehead creased. "Five years ago, on May 15, there was a farewell day for Sam Wooser." He shrugged. "It's barely interesting to *me* anymore."

"May 15," echoed Liza. "May 15. That was the day of the fire. The fire that took Jessie's life. When I was looking through Miss Violet's clippings, I saw the date."

"The fire was May 15, too?" asked Sam. "I'd forgotten. I left for Arizona right after the farewell party. I heard about the tragedy, of course, but weeks later."

He shook his head. "Terrible tragedy."

"Wait a minute," Liza said slowly. "The big pocket watch. Your gift from the staff. Was it running when you received it?"

"It sure was, and it was accurate, and it still is," Sam said. "Why?"

"The watch said twelve o'clock," Liza said softly. "But the article I read said the fire was in the morning. Jessie would have been dead by the time the picture was taken."

Chapter Nine

Jessie was dead when the picture was taken," Logan murmured.

"A picture of a ghost," said Liza.

"This is extraordinary!" Sam shook his head.

"Liza, did Miss Violet save the news article that told about the fire?" Logan asked.

Liza nodded. She stood up quickly and walked over to the box of clippings she had sorted. Then she began flipping nervously through them.

"Here it is," she said finally, her voice low. "May 15. The blaze was at eleven o'clock in the morning. Nineteen people were killed. Most of the bodies were unidentifiable."

She glanced up. "And there's another article." She leafed through some more clippings. "Here. Jessie's wife identified his body, and there was a memorial service." Liza hesitated. "Most of the bodies were unclaimed. No one cares about derelicts."

Logan stared at Liza. "So Jessie's wife could have identified the wrong body," he said.

"And Jessie could still be alive," Liza finished.

Sam ran his hand through his thinning hair. "I think you've hit on it, kids. Jessie didn't die in that fire. He came to the Brillstone, had his picture taken by accident, and then just disappeared."

"Why would someone pretend to be dead?" asked Liza.

"To get the insurance money," said Logan. "His wife identified a body and collected the money. Then the two of them went away and lived happily ever after on all that cash."

Liza nodded excitedly. "But then Jessie read about his aunt Violet's inheritance. It was mentioned in all the papers. And he and his wife decided to come back to try to get the money."

Sam looked at Logan and Liza. "Jessie couldn't risk letting Miss Violet know he was still alive. After all, he'd go to jail if anyone found out that he'd pretended to be dead just for the insurance. So they had to think up some scheme."

Liza broke in. "And the scheme was to get Bella Vine to convince Miss Violet that Jessie was talking to her from the spirit world—something like that. Then she might be convinced that she should give the money to the phony spiritualist group, the Seekers." She paused.

"But why would Jessie have been so stupid as to appear in public—at the Brillstone—when he was supposed to have been at the fire?" asked Liza. "Nobody's that dumb."

Logan reached into his pocket for his keys and jangled them. It always helped him think.

"Maybe he didn't know about the fire at the time," he said after a minute.

"But if he was going to pretend to be dead—" Liza began.

"This is what must have happened," said Logan. "Jessie and his wife had planned to pretend that he had been killed. But they were waiting for an accident—the kind of accident that would claim a lot of lives and make it difficult to identify bodies. And then the derelict hotel burned down. Maybe Jessie's wife heard about the fire on the radio or saw a news report on television. Meanwhile Jessie was over here at the Brillstone, looking for Miss Violet when she was out of town."

Sam nodded. "And then when Jessie got home, he heard about the fire. He remembered the photograph was taken but probably assumed that people wouldn't remember the exact time they'd seen him here."

Sam paused and then went on. "Besides, how would he ever guess that you could tell the time from a simple snapshot? And there was a good chance that no one noticed him when he was here—picture or no picture. There are always a lot of people coming and going in the Brillstone. For all Jessie knew, he was just a small blur in the background."

"But how did he know that Miss Violet had the snapshot?" Logan asked.

Liza leaned forward. "Miss Violet said she wrote to Jessie's wife after the fire. She told her that she had the photograph and treasured it. So

Jessie would have known about the picture for several years."

"But why couldn't Bella Vine have stolen it herself?" asked Logan. "Jessie would have told her about the picture. She was over at Miss Violet's many times."

"There are lots of pictures—dozens," Liza said. "It would be easier—and quicker—for Jessie to pick out the right one, I suppose. Bella Vine hadn't met Sam, remember. She wouldn't have known what he looked like."

The three of them sat quietly for a moment, their thoughts on Jessie, Bella Vine, and the strange happenings of the last few days.

"At least their scheme failed," said Logan, finally. "That's the good part. Miss Violet has given the check to Phyllis Baker for the Cat's Meow."

"And there's nothing Bella Vine or Jessie can do about it," said Liza with satisfaction.

Sam sighed deeply and stood up. "We can at least be thankful that Miss Violet got what she wanted, and that she's content." He chuckled. "And now that she's agreed to my proposal, I think she'll be more content than ever."

Logan and Liza exchanged glances.

"What proposal?" Liza asked.

"Two beautiful weeks in Arizona with my wife and me, all expenses paid," Sam said proudly. "It's one of the reasons I came back here. Jackie—that's my wife—misses Miss Violet awfully, and I didn't think a phone call would do the trick."

He looked warmly at Logan and Liza. "If we had the room, we'd have you, too. Well, enough said. I've got many things to get ready before our trip back to Arizona. We'll be leaving as soon as Miss Violet returns."

Logan and Liza shook hands with Sam and said goodbye.

"I'm sorry we thought you were a crook," Liza said.

Sam laughed.

As Logan and Liza started to leave Miss Violet's apartment, Liza caught something out of the corner of her eye. It was a large briefcase, propped against the far end of the couch.

"Oh, Logan, look," she said, pointing. "It's Phyllis Baker's briefcase. She must have left it here by mistake. I bet she's frantic without it."

She thought a moment. "Let's just call her to let her know we have it. We can take the briefcase over to your apartment and hold it for her."

"Sure thing," Logan agreed. "We can call her from there. Have you got her number?"

Liza shook her head. "I haven't any idea how to get in touch with her. Let me check Miss Violet's address book." She went back to the desk and leafed through a small book. "No luck," Liza sighed.

"Well, maybe her address and phone number are inside the briefcase," Logan suggested. "She probably has calling cards in it."

"Right," Liza said. "She must have three zillion brochures in here," she muttered as she picked up the briefcase. "It weighs a ton."

Liza opened the lid and stared.

"Logan!" she whispered hoarsely. "Look!"

Logan hurried over and squatted on the floor next to Liza. "I don't believe it," he said as Liza withdrew a large carpetbag from the briefcase.

She blinked as she opened it and pulled out a wig with cascading dark hair. Then she held up tubes and bottles of makeup. She and Logan stared into the bag at bunched-up clothing and a bright purple scarf. Dozens of bracelets lay among the dark folds of a skirt.

"Bella Vine's clothes," Liza whispered.

"What's this?" Logan asked, pulling out a thick, padded vest.

Liza stared at it. "I don't know. It just looks like a padded vest."

"What's all this junk of Bella Vine's doing in Phyllis Baker's briefcase?" Logan asked. And then his eyes met Liza's.

"Bella Vine and Phyllis Baker must be the same person," Liza said softly.

Logan still held the padded vest in his hand. "And this is how Bella Vine made herself look nearly twice as big as Phyllis." He set the vest back in the briefcase, and his hand touched something else. He pulled it out. A flat sandal. "And this is how she was short when she was Bella. As Phyllis she wore very high heels."

Liza shook her head, unable to take her eyes off the contents of the briefcase. "Phyllis Baker and Bella Vine are the same person. I can't believe it!"

Logan shook his head. "What a hoax!" He suddenly straightened. "Liza, Miss Violet gave her check to Phyllis Baker, which means she gave it to Bella Vine."

"Which means that Jessie will get it," Liza said. "We really goofed this time."

"Who could have guessed the two women were the same person?" Logan said. "How could she have changed her appearance so quickly?"

"She must be a quick-change artist, I guess," said Liza, pacing back and forth.

"But that time after the welcome home dinner," Logan said, "we saw Phyllis when she came to talk to Webb and then we saw Bella Vine a few minutes later at Miss Violet's. She couldn't have managed to change *that* quickly, could she?"

Liza stopped her pacing. "The elevator!" she said suddenly. "There were so many problems with it. Phyllis could have just pressed the stop button, changed clothes, and stepped out a few minutes later as Bella Vine."

"She must have changed on the roof, too," Logan said. "Remember, I followed her there after the seance. She had to change into Phyllis fast—before Miss Violet changed her mind about giving the money to the cat shelter."

He shivered, remembering the eerie encounter. "When I heard her calling to Jessie, I thought she was calling to a ghost. And then I followed him and lost him—"

He stopped excitedly. "Liza. That place—the place I followed Jessie to after he and Bella Vine

met on the roof. That's where Phyllis has gone—
to meet Jessie—with the check! If we can only get
to them before they get away!"

Liza sprang up. "What are we waiting for?
Doomsday? Let's go!"

Chapter Ten

There!" Logan stepped out of his car and pointed at a storefront. The fog had lifted, and in the morning light the building looked even grimier than before.

Liza stared at the faded sign on the window: "Majestic Theatrical Supplies."

"I followed Jessie right here," Logan said. "But then I lost track of him."

Logan and Liza silently approached the store. No lights were on inside.

The street was empty except for discarded cans and bits of rubbish. The wind caught pieces of yellowed newspaper and slammed them against the sides of buildings.

Suddenly there was a clanging noise. It seemed to Logan and Liza to come from somewhere nearby. They cautiously stepped closer to the building.

Then they heard another sound—one familiar to them both. Someone was whistling "Mary Had a Little Lamb." The tune floated softly on the damp, heavy air.

"It's Jessie!" Logan whispered. He and Liza stepped around the corner of the building and stared. A man stood with his back to them, emptying bags and bottles into a can at the side of the shop.

Logan pressed Liza's arm, and they silently approached him.

"Jessie?" Logan called.

The man spun around and stared at Logan and Liza. He looked from one to the other, his eyes wide.

Logan spoke more loudly. "Everything has been found out, Jessie. The police will be here soon."

A sound escaped Jessie's throat and he shook his head despairingly. "I knew it! I told Lorraine!

Why did I ever marry her after Helga died?" He seemed to be talking to himself.

"Coming back here was a mistake," Jessie moaned. "A horrible mistake!" His eyes darted around the vacant lot.

"You can make a run for it if you want to," Logan told him. "But it won't do you any good. The police will find you, you know that."

Jessie shook his head again. "I won't run. I know they've caught up with me." He paused, then shouted, "I was right, Lorraine! I was right! We should have stayed where we were."

Logan and Liza looked at each other. Was Lorraine another alias for Phyllis Baker and Bella Vine? A door swung softly shut. Jessie's wife must be in there.

Jessie turned back to Logan and Liza. "It's all her fault. She thought up the whole scheme. It was her idea to say the body of a bum was me. We needed that insurance money, sure, but we'd have managed somehow. We'd have borrowed again from Aunt Violet. But Lorraine made me do it. It's her fault," he whined. "She's the one. I just went along with her."

"And you went along with the scheme of pretending to be your spirit, raised from the dead, didn't you?" asked Liza. "Did Lorraine pretend to be Bella Vine?"

"Yes. What a stupid idea!" Jessie said. "Aunt Violet would never have believed in such nonsense. I tried to tell Lorraine that. But oh no, she knew better." He wiped his hand across his face. "I was trying to get the picture. The one of Sam and me. I knew his wife had taken one that day, and Aunt Violet wrote to my wife to say that she had it. It hadn't seemed important. But then I was back in town, and I found out that Sam was back, too. Lorraine said that Aunt Violet was making a scrapbook of all her pictures. I was afraid that she or Sam would put two and two together. What if they realized that I had been at the Brillstone *after* the fire?" He shook his head miserably.

"So you tried to get the picture after Bella Vine—Lorraine—left the door open, after the seance," said Liza.

"Yes, and I got it. I'd tried before. And it was the wrong apartment. I realized my mistake as soon as I looked through the desk. I hadn't realized that Aunt Violet had moved across the hall four years ago. I still had my old key."

That explains the intruder, thought Logan.

"I had to try again," said Jessie. He looked at his feet. "I got the picture. Lorraine said I did a good job and that I was the only one who could have done it, since she didn't know which picture was the important one."

"And Lorraine did a good job, too, persuading Miss Violet to give you all that money for a cat shelter," said Logan.

"What cat shelter?" Jessie asked, confused. "I don't know about any cat shelter or any money."

"The Cat's Meow," Liza said. "Your aunt gave a check to Phyllis Baker. That's Bella Vine. That's also Lorraine, your wife."

"Aunt Violet gave her money?" he asked incredulously.

"A lot," Logan said. "Your wife has the check now."

Jessie's mouth hung open. Suddenly he turned and ran toward the door. "Lorraine!" he shouted. "Lorraine! You lied! You got the money and you didn't even tell me! You said you couldn't get it."

Almost at the door, Jessie again shouted Lorraine's name. He wrenched the door open, and the grimy glass window in it rattled.

Liza was at his heels, and Logan was through the door an instant later.

The two of them stood in an almost empty apartment. There was only one room. A grayish sink seemed to serve as the kitchen. Unwashed cups and glasses sat on a counter next to it. On the far wall was an unmade bed. And in the middle of the room were two chairs and a small table. There were no other furnishings. Phyllis was nowhere to be seen.

Jessie was already lunging toward another door. He yanked it open. A gaping black hole seemed to lie beyond it. He hurled himself in and disappeared.

Logan and Liza made their careful way through the dark corridor. Peeling paint from the walls caught on their jackets. And then they suddenly came to another door. Jessie had left it partially open, and Logan could see into the dimly lit theatrical supplies shop.

Liza led the way into the store, gasping as she collided with a swinging mannequin.

"I know you're here, Lorraine. Now explain everything to me!" Jessie shouted as he ran through the shop.

Several mannequins swung slowly, turning their heads and swinging their arms. Their painted eyes seemed to stare menacingly.

"She's gone!" wailed Jessie. He tore to the dingy front door and fumbled with the lock. "She's gone! Taken the money and left me to the police!"

Logan glanced up at the balcony he had seen earlier. The two dressed mannequins were just as they had been, but he sensed a movement.

In an instant, Logan had crossed the floor. He stood at the bottom of the staircase and looked up. He could see a form huddled near the table.

He was going to start up the steps when something made him stop. He examined the bottom of the staircase. It was on wheels. He grabbed at the sides and pulled with all his strength. The staircase pulled away from the balcony, screeching wildly on the rusty wheels.

Lorraine stood up behind the balcony table and cursed.

"You've never been anything but trouble, Jessie!" Her face was coldly angry. "You've always leaned on me, expected me to plan everything, do everything, think of everything. And now look what you've done. We've been found out. All because of you. I did everything, and you loused it up!" Her voice was filled with contempt.

Logan and Liza watched, fascinated. Jessie's shoulders straightened. "Wait a minute, Lorraine. I never wanted to play dead. That was your idea. All of it. Just because of the money. Money! I could have got Aunt Violet to give me money as a loan. Then I wouldn't have the police after me now!"

"You're a pitiful excuse of a man, Jessie," Lorraine said angrily. "You've never been able to do anything right. All you had to do was to rent us a place for a couple of months. And this is what you come up with. This filthy hole with that stupid landlord lurking around—afraid of his own shadow, terrified that someone is going to rob him. Rob him of what?"

"Well, it was a safe place," said Jessie.

Lorraine laughed shrilly. "Safe! These kids have caught us. That's how safe it is!"

Liza tilted her head and stared up at Lorraine. This is the way she looked as Phyllis Baker, thought Liza—trim and neat, with pale, short hair.

"How did you turn into Bella Vine and back again to Phyllis Baker?" Liza found herself asking.

The woman shrugged. "It was a clever

masquerade, was it not? And it was also clever of me to establish a not-for-profit corporation. No one would have guessed that I'd just take the money and escape to another country."

"Not entirely," Liza said. "You left your briefcase in Miss Violet's apartment. When Logan and I opened it to find your telephone number, we found all of Bella Vine's clothes and makeup."

"See, Lorraine, see?" shouted Jessie triumphantly. "I'm not the only one who makes mistakes!"

Lorraine paid no attention to him. "I changed in the elevator and on the roof." She smiled coldly at Liza. "The elevator had been acting up, so one stop more or less didn't cause any alarm."

Logan spoke up impatiently. "When Miss Violet told Bella Vine that she wanted to give her money to Phyllis Baker for the cat shelter, you were anxious to change into Phyllis as soon as possible, right? Before she could change her mind."

Lorraine nodded. "It wasn't easy. I went up to the roof. That's where I'd arranged to meet Jessie, after he got the picture. When he showed it to me, I knew we were safe—no one could find out about our scheme. That's when I changed from Bella

Vine to Phyllis and went back to see Miss Violet. She was pleased and surprised to see me. She made out the check." Her expression changed. "And that would have been that, if it hadn't been for this stupid man."

"I've done a lot," said Jessie. "I got the picture!"

"Sure you did, and what happened? You let two kids follow you here. You're a dumb clown, Jessie." She glanced around, as though searching for a way to escape. Then she leaned over the railing and looked down. It was too far to jump.

Jessie shook his fist. "And what do you call what you are, Lorraine? You got Aunt Violet to give you her inheritance for some phony cause. A cat shelter. And you were going to go away with the money and leave me. Weren't you, Lorraine? Admit it!"

Her lip curled. "Whine, whine, whine. That's all you've ever done, Jessie."

"I'm glad you've been caught," said Jessie. "Glad, do you hear that? If I go to prison, so do you. And you thought you'd be off somewhere in the sunshine. Without me!"

He turned to Logan and Liza, his eyes rimmed with red. "She kept saying she was trying to get money for us. She pretended to Aunt Violet that she was a spiritualist so that Aunt Violet would give her money. Lorraine and I had planned to go to South America. But she didn't tell me about her other scheme. A cat shelter!" he spit out the words. Then he leaned over the counter and started to sob.

Liza couldn't help feeling sorry for him, even if he had been a crook—pretending he was dead so that he and his wife could collect the insurance money. After all, he was Miss Violet's nephew.

Thinking of Miss Violet reminded Liza that she was supposed to call.

"We've got to let Miss Violet know what's happened," she whispered to Logan. "I can reach her now at the number she gave me."

"I wonder what she'll say when she finds out that Jessie isn't dead, after all," said Logan.

"We'll see," promised Liza, reaching for the telephone.

When Miss Violet answered, Liza spoke quickly, explaining the events of the past hours.

"Oh my," said Miss Violet. "Oh my."

At first Liza thought Miss Violet was crying, but then she realized that she was laughing. "You tell Jessie that was a mean trick he pulled, but I'm glad he's alive. As for that Phyllis woman and Bella Vine—the same person? Think of that! What a performance, my dear. Very entertaining. Tell her I fell for it all hook, line, and sinker. She'll be needing some consolation, I expect."

Miss Violet chuckled. "What an extraordinary game! What extraordinary news! And now I have some news for you, dear. Not earthshaking news, but nice. I've looked into another animal shelter, just out of curiosity's sake. And it's established and wonderfully worthy. So now I can give my money to that one instead."

"How wonderful!" said Liza.

"But I'm not finished," said Miss Violet happily. "The best part of all is still to come. Sam Wooser and his wife are going to run the shelter! It's close enough for Bainbridge and me to visit once in a while. Isn't that lovely?"

"It's more than lovely," Liza agreed. "It's terrific!"

By the time Liza had said goodbye and hung up, Lorraine and Jessie were screaming at each other.

"I guess now I can call the police," said Logan.

"In a minute," said Liza. "There's something

I've been meaning to do ever since I got back from Seattle.''

She put her arms around Logan and kissed him.

Somehow Dan and the roses no longer seemed very important.

About the Authors Florence Parry Heide and Roxanne Heide have no trouble thinking of exciting adventures for the two Brillstone detectives. Often this mother-daughter team will drive to a family lakeside cottage in Wisconsin, spend several days with their typewriters, and emerge with the plot for a mystery. Several more day-long sessions, and a new story is ready.

Florence Heide brings versatility and enthusiasm to all she does. She's written lyrics for songs, picture books (including the highly acclaimed *The Shrinking of Treehorn*), short novels for teen readers, stories for reading programs and, of course, many popular mysteries. Roxanne Heide has produced picture books and textbook materials and has collaborated on fifteen mysteries in the Spotlight and Brillstone series, published by Albert Whitman.

Knowing her books are being read and enjoyed by children gives Florence Heide a special sense of accomplishment. When Wisconsin schoolchildren in grades four through eight cast their votes, Florence Heide became the winner of the Golden Archer Award for 1977. Among her titles mentioned time and again were *Mystery at MacAdoo Zoo* and *Mystery of the Bewitched Bookmobile*.

DATE DUE

SEP 17 '85			
SEP 24 '85			
MAY 6 '86			
OCT 20 '86			
OCT 27 '86			
MAY 12 '88			
DEC 10 '90			
FEB 18 '91			
APR 26 '93			
NOV 20 '96			
DEC 14 '01			
SEP 9 '03			